To Larae,

Dream the impossible!

SCROLLS OF ZNDARIA

SCROLL 1
THE GOLDEN WIZARD

J.S. JAEGER

Illustrated by:
Jared Beckstrand

Synergy-Books Publishing

Scrolls of Zndaria—Scroll One: The Golden Wizard

By Jerry D. and Stephanie R. Jaeger

Synergy Books Publishing
www.synergy-books.com
PO Box 911232
St. George, UT 84791

Illustrated by: Jared Beckstrand

ISBN: 978-0-9885608-0-2 (Soft Cover Edition)

ISBN: 978-0-9885608-1-9 (Hard Cover Edition)

ISBN: 978-0-9885608-2-6 (Electronic Edition)

Dedication

Dedicated to Jessica, Amanda, Tyler, and
Kassidy. We love you!

Acknowledgements

Seven years ago, we had no idea what we were getting ourselves into when we decided to write a book. It all started when Jerry envisioned the magical world of Zndaria. We could not have done this on our own.

Thank you, David and Delilah Jaeger for being with us as we sorted out a new twist in our lives. David, thanks for your research on the rooms of the Red Wizard's tower and for being Jerry's sounding board. Delilah, your early advice put *Scrolls of Zndaria* on the right path and helped us see the wisdom in working as co-authors.

Thank you to our editor, Caroll Shreeve. Your ability to see what was missing and communicate that to us has been invaluable. Your positive attitude and encouragement gave us an extra boost of energy as we pushed through to the end.

Also thank you, Summer Romney, Rhea Racker, and Jennifer Racker for editing and reviewing our manuscript.

Thank you, David W. Smith, owner of Synergy Publishing, for introducing us to Caroll and helping us get our book in print.

Thank you, Jared Beckstrand for bringing our characters to life.

Thank you to our friends and family who have encouraged us along the way.

The biggest thank you goes to our daughters, Jessica and Amanda. Your sacrificed family time on weekends and holidays so your parents could work on "the book" has not gone unnoticed. We couldn't have done this without your countless hours of babysitting Tyler and Kassidy and for your editing and suggestions along the way.

Chapters

Chapter One

A TOUGH LIFE

Nathanial "Nate" McGray, a lanky fifteen-year-old boy, pounded along the dirt road leaving a wake of dust. A glance over his shoulder confirmed the bullies were not far behind. Mustering all his strength, Nate ignored the intense burning in his legs and sprinted even faster. The sight of the bridge brought a flicker of hope—escape into the Darkoak Forest was near!

Three thugs scrambled out of the ravine, blocking Nate's path. Fighting off a wave of panic, Nate lunged at a gangling elf with curly black hair. They toppled onto the cobblestone bridge. Nate attempted to scramble away. The elf grasped Nate's foot long enough for his cohorts—a red-headed, freckle-faced dwarf and a baby-faced, beefy young man—to seize Nate's upper arms and yank him to his feet. They turned him around just as Derik—an abnormally tall, flabby seventeen-year-old human—reached the bridge with the rest of his gang.

"Caught . . . you!" Derik panted, wiping his shirt sleeve across his sweating bald head. "We have a . . . surprise for you! Let's go!"

Nate thrashed in protest. His captors tightened their grips and dragged him into a secluded area within the trees.

"How do you like flirgoo?" Derik leered. He nodded to a spiky-haired halfling. With a snicker, the halfling retrieved a wooden bucket from behind a thick mulberry bush. Tilting it mischievously toward Nate, he revealed its contents—red flammable sap from a flirgrossa tree.

"W-w-what're you going to do with that?" Nate cringed.

"You're about to become The Great Flirgoo Wizard!" Derik mocked. He grabbed Nate's hair.

In a coordinated strike that surprised even himself, Nate jerked his head free and kneed Derik in the groin. Derik stumbled backward. Tripping over a raised root, he crashed with a screech into the mulberry bush. The gang erupted with laughter. Nate grinned.

Smeared with purple juice, Derik pulled himself out of the bush. "Shut up, you punkler nicklers!" Derik ordered. "Step on his feet!"

Derik stormed toward Nate with clenched fists. His face was bright red. A vein pulsed in his neck. He slugged Nate in the stomach, hard. The bullies lost their grip. Nate dropped to his knees and gasped for breath.

Derik yanked Nate's shirt over his head. "Hold him still!"

Despite Nate's squirming, Derik and the halfling used bark to smear flirgoo on Nate's back and chest. Then Derik, the two elves, and the baby-faced young man each grabbed one of Nate's limbs.

"Oh Great Flirgoo Wizard, what shall we do with thee?" they chanted sarcastically.

"Put me down you idiots!" Nate struggled to break free.

They carried him ceremoniously from the cover of the trees. Guffawing, the gang continued their charade, marching toward a bloated, moss-covered stump rooted on the embankment near the bridge.

"Great Flirgoo Wizard, receive thy throne!" They chortled wildly, wedging Nate into the decaying log until only his skinny legs flailed out of the stump.

"Get m-m-me out!" Nate hollered. His frenzied scream echoed inside the log. In an instant, tiny, fiery lights lit up all around him. Nate realized, with alarm, he'd disturbed a nest of fire wasps.

"Hope you know a good spell to get out of there," Derik taunted. He kicked the log. The fire wasps swarmed menacingly around Nate.

"H-h-help me!" Nate pled. A fire wasp embedded itself in the flirgoo on Nate and exploded. Screaming in pain, Nate called for help again, stopping only when he heard indistinct arguing.

With a swift yank on his legs, Nate was freed from the stump right when another wasp exploded. Stumbling backward, Nate was grateful to see his older brother—Ted, Ted's best friend—an elf named Nordof, and another shorter elf Nate didn't recognize. They ducked to avoid a cluster of fire wasps raging out of the narrow opening.

Ted—a stockier version of Nate with brown eyes, short golden blond hair, and the large, distinguished McGray snout—bolted down the road after the bullies. Nate and the others followed. They easily caught up to them.

"Hey ya dorker, what were ya doin' ta my brother?" Ted challenged Derik.

"We were just having some fun with the wannabe wizard." Derik clenched his fists and looked down his nose at Ted, "Why do you care?"

"Cuz I'm the only one who treats my brother that way!" Ted insisted.

They circled around each other, fists poised to fight. Everyone else surrounded them, roughly jockeying for the best view. Nate fought his way in from the edge of the circle.

The sound of approaching horses made everyone freeze.

"Well, well, well, if it isn't two of Burrowville's most infamous troublemakers." A young knight approached the crowd with another knight on horseback. He eyed Derik and Ted. "What's going on here?"

Ted and Derik lowered their fists slightly. No one else moved or responded.

"I said, what's going on here?" The young knight demanded, straightening up on his horse. After a brief silence, he declared, "Looks like we might have to escort some of you home for disturbing the . . ."

"Ah, just let them fight," the older, pudgy knight interjected in a gruff voice, waving off the other knight's look of contempt.

This was all the encouragement Derik needed. With a wild swing, Derik connected with Ted's cheekbone, knocking him to his knees.

Grasping Derik's pants, Ted pulled himself up, exposing Derik's red satiny underwear. With Nate cheering him on, Ted redirected all of his weight and drove his head into Derik's flabby belly.

"Blaaaaaaaaaaaah," Derik gagged. He lost his breakfast with such force that the vomit ricocheted off Ted's back.

Nate, and everyone else in the circle, was splattered with regurgitated onions and spicy hog. The revolting smell hung in the air. Chaos prevailed. Everyone, including the knights, scattered. The baby-faced young man rushed past Nate, shoving him in the chest.

Nate's feet flew out from under him. He landed on his back with a thud, striking his head on a rock. Bright lights flashed in his eyes. Drums pounded inside his skull. He willed his body to move, but it laid still. His world went black.

Chapter Two

AN ENCHANTED MURAL

I hate bullies. Nate moaned to himself. He opened his eyes and sat up on a cot. "Where am I?"

Sunlight poured through a stained-glass window. The round room was warm. Rock walls made Nate feel like he was in a cave. From the grey stone ceiling, water fell like rain into a slick black wash basin.

The vomit and flirgoo were gone. Yumber leaves covered the welts on his torso. A hardened paste protected the lump on the back of his head. He didn't feel any pain.

"How are you doing?" The unfamiliar elf who'd helped rescue him earlier stood in the doorway.

"I've never felt better!"

"I'm not surprised. My mother's the best handmaiden around." The elf handed Nate a shirt. "Good thing she had her dragon soap. That sap is sticky stuff."

"Dragon soap?"

"It's made from red dragon scales. It'll clean almost anything off in no time."

"Nice!" Nate slipped the shirt over his head. "I haven't seen you around before. Who are you?"

"I'm Danzandorian Mockorilian Gordenall the Fourth." Danzandorian's green eyes hinted that he relished Nate's look of surprise. "But you can call me Blinkly."

"Blinkly?"

"Unless you prefer Danzandorian?"

"Oh, no!" Nate insisted. "Blinkly is fine. How did I get here?"

"Your brother and my cousin, Nordof, helped carry you to my home. Come on, I'll show you my room."

Nate smelled fresh rain and pine. He followed Blinkly through the doorway into a small clearing. They were surrounded by a forest of red, green, and blue pine trees. The fragrant pines brushed against the unusually high azure ceiling. Several blue lily birds with bright orange wings chirped gleefully, swooping between the trees. A stream babbled along the edge of the clearing.

"Do you like the changes we've made in here?" Blinkly asked. "It's the old Flanhare place."

"Really?" Nate pictured the two-story, red timber-framed house offset by crumbling pale daub panels. "But how?"

"Elfish magic," Blinkly stated proudly. He led Nate to a green pine across the clearing. "Why'd those bullies attack you anyway?"

Nate thought of the trouble he'd already caused. "I blurted out that I want to be a wizard someday," he shrugged.

"A wizard? That's great!" Blinkly started up a spiral staircase fashioned from the tree's boughs.

"Yeah, but it's impossible." Nate curiously eyed Blinkly, the first one to ever show support of a dream even Nate's parents insisted was a foolish notion. "You're not from around here are you?" Nate worked his way up the tree trunk.

"Nope, my mother and I just arrived a few days ago."

A tailless, green, four-legged creature with bulging eyes jumped between the branches near Nate.

"Here in Burrowville," Nate explained, "unless you're nobility, you have two choices—follow in the trade of your father or join the military." The critter jumped to a red pine and turned red. Nate gasped.

"And your father's not a wizard."

"Not even close. He's the king's woodsman."

"From their training this morning, I'm guessing your brother and Nordof are taking the military route."

"Yep, the tryouts are in a couple of weeks. If Ted has his way, he'll be the next champion." The creature leaped to a blue pine. Its skin changed to match the tree. At the top of the staircase, they reached a door. "Your house is unbelievable!"

"Thanks, but now for the best part!" Stepping through the door, Blinkly spread his arms open.

Nate was flabbergasted. Red water spouted from the mouth of a life-sized black stone dragon head mounted on the far wall. The water hit the floor and separated into two streams, creating an island in the center of the room. A golden bridge allowed access across the moat to a large feather bed covered by a fluffy, forest-green quilt.

One wall held an arsenal of weapons. Daggers, swords, hatchets, maces, javelins, and bows surrounded a suit of armor that looked like it would fit Blinkly.

A three-dimensional picture depicting a beautiful, serene forest of the same colorful pines from downstairs dominated another wall. Framed in thick, deep brown wood, the mural was filled with mystical creatures. A herd of unicorns grazed regally in a sunny meadow of wild grass. Hundreds of fairies playfully darted around the trunks of the swaying trees and colorful lily birds fluttered among the branches.

"They're moving!" Nate gasped in awe.

"Of course, it's a living painting!"

"It's alive?"

"Not exactly," Blinkly explained. "It was created from the branches of an enchanted tree. We can see everything the tree has seen. This is the forest where I grew up."

"It's beautiful!" Nate exclaimed.

"It used to be. Now it's nothing more than a deathly wasteland."

"What do you mean?" Nate walked up to examine the mural more closely. Beneath a row of golden rings, the bottom of the frame was lined with a row of golden suns.

"I'll show you." Blinkly joined Nate. "There is a ring for every year and a sun for every day the tree has lived." He pressed the last golden ring and a sun toward the middle of the frame. The mural turned dark and dreary—engulfed by a gloomy mist. The colorful, lush trees were now charcoal and bare. Tall, gnarly weeds had overrun the serene meadow. The forest was void

13

of mystical creatures. Everything seemed lifeless. "That's my home today," Blinkly said with disgust.

Staring at the cold and uninviting landscape, Nate shivered. Suddenly, an extremely ugly creature landed on a dead tree branch within the painting. Nate jumped back in shock. He had never seen a harpy before. Terrified, he gaped at the sharp, piercing talons, the contorted body of a vulture, and the skinny, ragged face of an old witch.

"That's wicked," Nate mumbled.

"That's nothing compared to King Siddon."

"King who?" Nate looked up.

"King Siddon—the king of the Riders." Blinkly's body tensed.

"Never heard of him."

"King Siddon," Blinkly said the name through gritted teeth, "has declared his intention to rule Zndaria. He controls a vast army of devilish warriors, destroyed my home, and continues to march against any kingdom that refuses to join him."

"Oh."

"Do you want to see him?"

"Uh . . . I guess." Nate wasn't so sure.

Blinkly touched the third to the last ring and one of the suns at the end of the row. When the mural's beauty returned, he started for the door.

"I've promised my mother I wouldn't watch it anymore. I'll wait for you downstairs. You can't miss King Siddon, he's the tall, ugly elf."

Blinkly closed the door. Nate turned back to the mural. A flock of lily birds burst out of the trees, startled by a herd of shimmering, white unicorns led by a golden unicorn. The herd dashed through the meadow into the forest, bolting past an army positioning itself for battle.

Appearing ready to defend their kingdom, countless elves armed with long bows and dwarfs bearing crossbows stood strategically in the trees behind their king. Standing a head taller than an average dwarf, the armor-clad king stepped into the meadow, sunlight glistening off his brilliant golden crown. He had long brown hair, a thick, chest-length beard, and hefted a massive war hammer.

Across the meadow, a curiously tall, scrawny elf, whom Nate immediately assumed was King Siddon, appeared. Draped around his mesh armor, his dark green cloak left his bony fingers, coarse red hair, and rust-colored face exposed. A scar extended from the bottom of his pointy right ear and circled beneath his face, ending at the tip of his bony chin. Although his body seemed frail and he carried no weapons, his stance demanded respect. His steely, black eyes caused a sinister shiver to rush through Nate's body.

Behind their leader, several hooded elves in dark mesh armor rode slick black lions with blood-red manes. Each bore a flail that sported a spiked, steel ball.

A dark mist ravaged the landscape, blocking out the sun. Within the forest, the leaves of the surrounding trees fell to the ground, their withering branches fading to a charcoal grey. With his entourage waiting at the edge of the meadow, King Siddon advanced. The golden grass browned; noxious weeds overtook the meadow.

Stopping a few strides away from the dwarf king, King Siddon pointed his finger and appeared to make a demand. Although there was no sound, Nate felt a sense of pride when the dwarf uttered something and defiantly thrust his war hammer in the air. Suddenly the hammer disappeared, reappearing in Siddon's right hand. Siddon shot a ball of energy out of his left hand, engulfing the dwarf king in a dark cloud. When the smoke dissipated, the dwarf was gone.

The dwarf king's soldiers released their weapons. King Siddon and his Riders swept their cloaks over themselves and their lions. The arrows and bolts disintegrated upon impact.

King Siddon sneered and pointed across the meadow. Nate read his lips—"Attack!"

Hordes of devilish imps joined the charging Riders. The rust-skinned monsters varied in size, shape, and species. Some walked on two legs, others crawled on eight. Some had horns on their heads, others had floppy ears. Some carried menacing weapons, others gnashed their teeth and swiped their claws.

The evil army attacked with such vengeance the defenders didn't stand a chance. Nate raised his hand to his mouth. He suppressed a gag.

Running from the room, he slammed the door behind him and waited until his body stopped shaking. In shock, he slowly went down the stairs.

"So, what'd you think?" Blinkly seemed reluctant to ask.

Nate jumped, not realizing he'd reached the bottom step. "Uh . . ." Nate hesitated. How could he say it was the most disturbing thing he'd ever seen?

As if reading Nate's mind, Blinkly said, "Now you know why I'm not supposed to watch it anymore."

Just then a simply dressed elf walked around the corner. "Would you care for some fruit?" She offered them a selection from the bowl she carried.

Normally, Nate would have jumped at the chance to try new and exotic fruit, but right now he was just hoping his breakfast would stay in his stomach. "No, thank you," he mumbled.

"Sure, Sarima." Blinkly grabbed a rainbow-colored, star-shaped fruit.

Sarima nodded then walked away.

"Is that your mother?"

"Oh no, that's our maidservant. Come on," Blinkly crossed the clearing, "I'll introduce you to my mother."

Nate followed Blinkly to what appeared to be a solid red pine tree. Blinkly twisted a knot in the tree. A bulky door swung open.

"This is her garden room." Blinkly stepped inside.

Nate followed. He was surrounded by more floral varieties than he recognized or could even count. He marveled at stunning purple roses, bright orange tulips, giant turquoise daffodils, and dainty, golden daisies. In the center of the garden room, a striking, middle-aged elf, her elaborate golden braid dangling down her back, knelt next to several tiny, grey plants.

After acknowledging their presence with a nod, Blinkly's mother began to sing. Nate watched in disbelief. As if dancing, the stems of the dull plants grew taller, climbing high into the air. Several soft violet leaves unfurled. Five glimmering, silver petals stretched out into a glorious blossom.

Blinkly's mother stopped singing and rose. Her brown wool dress extended to her wrists and flowed down to her ankles. Walking lightly in black slip-on shoes, she carried herself with a dignity that surprised Nate. Her perfect, emerald-green eyes sparkled. Nate resisted the urge to bow.

"Danzandorian!" Blinkly's mother embraced him briefly. "Who's your friend?"

"This is Nate. Nate, this is my mother, Laonia Gordenall."

"Welcome to our home." Lady Gordenall said. "Does your family live around here?"

"Oh no, we live across the bridge in the Darkoak Forest," Nate said. He didn't allow his face to betray his thoughts. *You probably couldn't get further from the rich side of town if you tried.*

Blinkly finished eating his rainbow fruit. "I'll be home for dinner, Mother."

"Very well. Nate, I look forward to meeting your family."

"They'll want to meet you, too. Thank you for cleaning me up." Nate gestured to his torso.

Blinkly started to the front door. "Come on, Nate. There's something unbelievable you have to see."

Following Blinkly down the rickety steps, Nate glanced back, still reeling from everything he'd seen inside. It was definitely Widow Flanhare's old place. Nothing on the outside had changed. *What could he possibly show me that's better than this?*

Chapter Three

TRESPASSERS BEWARE

Nate rushed behind Blinkly toward the blue marbled, four-story infirmary. "What are we doing here?"

"You'll see. It's hilarious." Blinkly started along the dirt trail that paralleled the outer wall, avoiding the iron gates and stone path that led visitors to the main entrance on the second floor.

Blinkly slowed to a walk before stopping near the back corner. "Hoist me up," he insisted.

"Okay?" Nate muttered with uncertainty. Scooping up Blinkly's waiting foot with interlocked fingers, Nate leaned backward. He raised Blinkly to the top of the wall.

"See you at the back door." Blinkly disappeared so suddenly that Nate stumbled backward, nearly falling down.

Nate steadied himself and looked around. "Blinkly?" There was no response. He jumped to grab the edge of the wall several boot-lengths over his head and scurried up until his stomach rested on top. Scanning the infirmary grounds, Nate noticed Blinkly at the back door waving for him to hurry.

Lowering himself over the wall, Nate dropped to the ground, carefully working his way through a garden filled with lush, colorful herbs. He cut across a winding walkway that snaked through clusters of bulky trees, flower patches, and well-trimmed grass. Rounding a quaint, white gazebo framed with vibrant purple roses, he joined Blinkly.

"How'd you get over the wall and through the garden so fast?" Nate asked.

"I blinked."

"You what?"

"I blinked. I can teleport myself short distances. That's why my friends call me Blinkly. Now be quiet and follow me." He pushed the door open and slipped inside.

To Nate, creeping down the hushed, sterile hallway felt like he was disturbing someone's peace. The brightly-lit torches lining the stark white walls added to his discomfort. They heard approaching footsteps and ducked inside an arched doorway.

Met with a pungent stench, Nate immediately knew they were in the mortuary. From plain, wooden boxes to fancy gem-encrusted golden caskets, a variety of coffins lined the walls or rested on tables. Covering his nose with the crook of his arm, Nate attempted to ignore the odor of death. He carefully zigzagged through the room.

Near the last few tables, Blinkly stopped at an emerald green coffin and motioned for Nate to join him. A small, hairy arm hung limply over the side. Peering in with reluctant curiosity, Nate spied an old grey-haired halfling lying on his back.

In a hoarse whisper, Blinkly said "I wonder what happened to . . ."

Suddenly the halfling rolled onto his side. Blinkly jumped back into the table behind him, almost knocking over a crystal coffin big enough to hold a grown human.

"He's alive!" Blinkly gasped.

"Of course he is," Nate chided quietly. "He's the undertaker."

"Oh," Blinkly's face colored slightly. "Well, he looks old enough to be dead. Come on," he whispered. "We're almost there." Blinkly and Nate picked their way through the remaining tables. Blinkly peeked into the hallway. "It's clear, let's go."

Nate followed Blinkly out of the mortuary and up the stairs to the main floor. After confirming no one was around, they rushed down another hallway and slipped into a room.

Dazzling sunlight flooded through breezy, blue curtains covering an expansive, oval window.

Landscape paintings hung on the walls. A bouquet of fresh lilies sat next to a bowl of red berries on a corner table. Nate's eyes were drawn to the one patient on three adjoining beds beneath the window.

"Holy b-b-blubber," Nate gasped. "I never knew someone could be so fat."

The middle bed supported most of the patient's body. The other two beds supported his outstretched, oversized arms, legs, and the excess fat from his torso. His stomach reminded Nate of their heifer just before she gave birth, only this belly was twice as big and had several more rolls of fat. A wool blanket draped the lower half of the body, but the feet stuck out like overgrown piglets.

"Who's 'ere?" The patient mumbled.

"Thorton?" Nate gasped. Moving to the side of the bed so he could see past the massive stomach, Nate gaped at the puffy, swollen head that barely resembled Thorton Brade.

Thorton turned his head and glared angrily at Nate. "You're no' 'upposed to be 'n here," he slurred through swollen lips.

"What happened?" Nate poked Thorton's bulging belly.

"Jus' ge' ou'!" Thorton ordered. His body jerked in an effort to get away from Nate.

"Come on, you've got to tell us what happened—then we'll leave, we promise." Nate stifled a laugh.

"'Elp! 'elp!" Thorton yelled.

Blinkly peeked out the door then hurried past Nate. "A handmaiden is coming. We'd better go." Reaching the head of the bed, Blinkly pulled himself up onto the mattress and onto the windowsill. "See you outside." He disappeared.

Nate heaved himself onto the bed. Thorton flailed his pudgy arms in what appeared to be a miserable attempt to grab him. "You better stop before you hurt yourself." Nate patted Thorton's inflated forehead teasingly.

"Don' 'ouch me!" Thorton jerked his head away.

"See you round, Thorton," Nate chuckled. He climbed onto the windowsill, lowered himself carefully off the ledge, and dropped down next to

Blinkly. Running to the front of the infirmary, they escaped out the gates.

"I thought my day was bad." Nate laughed. "What happened to him?"

"Well," Blinkly slowed his pace. "Last night I came to see my mother at work. I followed several knights rushing that boy up the stairs. With each of their steps, the boy's clothes stretched tighter and tighter. They turned him on his side to get him through the door. Just as they laid him on the beds his clothes *exploded*! I had to duck because a piece of his pants just missed me."

"Ugh! What made him grow like that?" Nate kept pace with Blinkly.

"I'm getting there. I overheard one of the knights say they found him outside the Red Wizard's tower—wailing and swelling. He tried to sneak in to see the Wizard but got hexed instead."

"Derik tried earlier this year."

"Derik? The bully?"

"Yep. My father saw him running out of the tower wearing next to nothing. He was covered in nasty blue slime and smelled awful. It was the second year that he'd failed the military tryouts

so I figured he was hoping to get the Wizard's
help."

"I can't think of anything worth breaching a
wizard's tower." Blinkly shook his head.

"Me neither." Nate refused to admit that he'd
considered it many times, but was never brave
enough to enter.

Chapter Four

BANNER DAY

The next morning, Main Street was lined with hundreds of spirited townsfolk, ripe with excitement. Ignoring nasty glares, Nate and Blinkly squeezed through the crowd until they arrived near the front. From this ideal location, Nate eagerly scanned his surroundings. Banner Day was the annual gathering of the King's

Council. To Nate, it was one of the few exciting things that happened in Burrowville. In years past, he'd spent most of the morning watching the grand procession of arriving nobles.

"Razzle! We missed one!" Nate muttered mostly to himself. A dwarf lord and his entourage had already started up the hill toward the White Castle. Almost immediately, intense cheering from down the street drew his attention.

Straining to see past a knight sauntering dutifully along the edge of the spectators, Nate spied the object of the commotion. Secured to the tip of a lance, a red silk banner embroidered with a crimson redwood tree was carried proudly by a young elf riding a white stallion. Following several horse lengths behind, the Redwood Elf Lord and his warriors were dressed in their finest bark armor. They carried magically woven leaf shields and bore exquisitely hand-crafted bows—all fashioned from the mighty redwood.

Over the noisy crowd, Nate yelled to Blinkly, "My sister, Denya, is studying with them to become a handmaiden."

"That's great, but she'd learn a lot more if she studied with the Pinetree Elves. No one understands healing like we do."

Before Nate could respond, a middle-aged lady with frizzy, red hair, who had been standing behind Blinkly, pushed past them and ran out into the middle of the road. Facing the elves, she threw open her arms and dropped to her knees.

"Marry me, Lord!" she shouted.

In a flash, two knights grabbed her despite her protesting kicks.

"Unhand me, he is my destiny!" she screamed. Stiffening her legs, she dug her heels into the ground, marking her course with two deep ruts while the knights dragged her away.

"She's crazy!" Blinkly chuckled. The Redwood Elves continued passed them.

"Yeah, every year we get a few fanatics," Nate shrugged.

The crowd started cheering. A gnome atop a majestic, white stag presented the banner for the Ice Gnomes from the Northern Tundra. Sparkling in the breeze, ice crystals decorated the dark-blue silk banner fastened to an ice spear. The Ice

Gnome Baroness—wearing a shimmering silver gown, a sapphire necklace, and an ice-crystal tiara—followed the banner in a stag-drawn crystal chariot. Her gnome warriors, donning crystal breastplates and ice daggers, rode reverentially behind her on splendid grey wolves.

"If this is all there is, Banner Day is boring," Blinkly said when they passed.

"Well, there's also a festival," Nate suggested. *How can he think this is boring?*

"Sounds great, let's go."

Nate worked his way through the crowd. Almost tripping over an old dwarf's cane, he shrugged apologetically. When he was finally free of the mob, he took off running with Blinkly close behind.

The dirt field near the castle was filled with tents of varying sizes and colors. Nate inhaled deeply.

Blinkly raised an eyebrow.

"Can't you smell it?" Nate grinned sheepishly. They rounded the corner to the front of a bright pink tent. Nate beamed, "Chocolateberry pie!"

The flaps of the tent were drawn open around a long, wooden table covered with rows of pies. Inside the tent, halflings with deep-brown skin baked pies in iron ovens. The table sign read:

**CHOCOLATEBERRY PIES
A TREAT FIT FOR A KING
5 BRONZE BITS EACH OR
TODAY'S SPECIAL –
THREE PIES FOR 1 SILVER BIT**

"So, are you going to buy one?" Blinkly nudged Nate.

"Nah, I only have three bronze bits," Nate sighed.

"I'll buy you one then." Blinkly reached into his pocket and felt around. "Drat! I forgot my pouch. Let's run home and get it."

"I'm fine." Nate knew he couldn't pay his friend back. He started to turn away from the pies when something sweeter caught his eye—Marnia.

Marnia, a young lady with curly blonde hair, aqua-blue eyes, and golden, tan skin, was the most beautiful girl in town. She strolled up to the table with two of her girlfriends—a chubby redheaded dwarf and a tall, skinny elf with long brunette hair. She ordered a pie.

"Hi, M-M-Marnia," Nate stammered before he could stop himself. He had adored her from afar for the past year, but had never spoken to her.

"Are you talking to me, Stutter-boy?" Marnia tossed her curls and turned to face Nate.

"Um, y-y-yeah." Nate's face burned.

"Listen Stutter-boy, I don't talk to nobodies. You may think you're going to be a great wizard someday, but you're not. You're a poor nobody and that's all you'll ever be." Marnia whirled away and faced the table. The other two girls snickered.

"Uh . . ." Lost for words, Nate stood paralyzed, feeling extremely stupid.

"Don't mind her, Nate," Blinkly jumped in. "She's just in pain because that nasty boil on her forehead is about to explode. We'd better get out of here if we don't want to get sprayed." Blinkly grabbed Nate by the arm and pulled him away, leaving Marnia and her friends standing with their mouths wide open.

For the rest of the morning, Blinkly and Nate wandered around the festival, weaving in and out of the tents. They drooled over exotic treats, unique crafts, and fancy trinkets. They were amazed by a six-armed jester who simultaneously juggled four axes, six swords, and ten knives. They marveled when a hill giant, who stood twice as tall as Nate, heaved a wagon full of spectators high above his head.

At a rainbow-striped tent where strings of beads draped over the entrance, Nate was tempted to get his fortune told by an old gypsy woman. When a young dwarf ahead of them was told that he would have a miserable year of death and despair, he quickly changed his mind.

"That's what you get when you let someone else determine your future," Blinkly chuckled, stepping back outside. A crowd of spectators had gathered in front of a huge cage draped with a green curtain. "What's going on over there?"

"I don't know, but we need to get to the magic show."

"We won't take long, I promise." Blinkly joined the crowd. Nate heard snarling behind the curtain.

"Step this way! See the most hideous creature ever!" bellowed a burly man with a tangled, red beard dressed from head to foot in fur clothes. He pulled a rope at the corner of the cage. The curtain lifted to reveal a vicious beast.

Practically filling the cage, the three-headed animal had the body of a lion, giant eagle wings, and the tail of a scorpion. Thrashing wildly, the beast snarled. Its bear, wolf, and bull teeth gnashed. It lunged at the crowd. They jumped back in fear.

"Teach this beast a lesson! Five tomatoes for two bronze bits," the man roared. Several townsfolk eagerly rushed up. He leered.

"This isn't right!" Blinkly looked angry. "No animal should be treated like this."

A teenaged dwarf threw the first tomato. It nailed the creature directly between the bull eyes. The beast roared.

"That's not an animal, it's a monster. Just look at it," Nate said.

"No! King Siddon is a monster. This is a helpless creature that is being provoked." Blinkly punched his open hand.

"But, there's nothing we can do about it. Besides, the magic show's about to start and that's the main reason I come to the festival." Nate turned to walk toward the larger sky-blue tent in the center of the field. Having only taken a few steps, he turned around. Blinkly still stared at the cage. "Come on, Blinkly. If we don't go now, we'll miss the show!"

Blinkly hesitated briefly, casting another glance at the beast before joining Nate.

Nate breathed a sigh of relief and they rushed to the magic show.

Chapter Five

MAGICAL MISHAPS

"Two, please." Nate handed two bits to a dark-skinned elf.

"Welcome to the magic show." She took the bits and winked at Blinkly.

Blinkly smiled and winked back. Walking toward the entrance he said to Nate, "She likes me."

"Yeah, but she'll be gone tomorrow," Nate chuckled. They entered the tent.

Inside, the noise was deafening. Rows of wooden benches were filled with hundreds of chattering townsfolk. Nate spotted two seats on the opposite side of the tent. He started toward them, but noticed they'd be sitting right in front of Derik and his snooty gang.

"I see two spots," Blinkly spoke over the crowd.

With a sigh of relief, Nate followed Blinkly down the aisle to the front of the stage. Stepping around two young halfling boys wrestling on the floor, Nate sat down next to their mother who struggled to console a screaming baby. Their father sat drinking a tall mug of intoxicating bubbler. Suddenly, the father looked up and met Nate's gaze. Quickly diverting his eyes, Nate shrugged. *Beats sitting by Derik.*

"Your attention please," a very thin man, whose brown hair was pulled into a long ponytail, bellowed in an attempt to silence the crowd. "The show is about to start . . . QUIET!" The chatter continued.

SHAAAAAAAAAAAAAAAAAAABOOM!

The ground shook. Brilliant blue smoke filled the stage. Everyone—including the baby halfling—fell silent. When the smoke dissipated, a plump, middle-aged man in a silky blue gown and matching cape stood on stage. In a clumsy bow, he scooped up his fallen pointed hat and placed it over his bald spot.

"Azuba—Cram," the magician yelled and opened his cupped hands. Pink, purple, and light-green doves flew out over the audience. "Welcome to the greatest magic show you'll ever see!" he bellowed.

The crowd cheered. The birds flew back to the stage and disappeared behind the curtain.

"Alla—Zalla—Estella," the magician shouted, twirling his wrists in the air.

An animated golden rod crowned with a green gem poked out from behind the curtain. Making a grand entrance, it hopped out onto the stage, flipped into the air, and landed directly in the magician's hand. When the magician tapped the floor with the tip of his staff, a round brass table strutted out from behind the curtain to the middle of the stage. Four matching chairs tap danced out to surround the table. The crowd whistled in approval. The magician moved to the edge of the stage.

"For my next act, I suggest you hold onto your seats. This show is about to take off." Holding his staff in front of him with both hands, the magician screamed, "Andia—Molas—Afay!"

All the benches in the tent began to shake. The magician slowly raised his staff in front of him. The benches began to levitate. Grabbing the edges of their seats, members of the audience squealed with excitement. Their seats followed the motion of the magician's staff—first rising several boot-lengths off the ground, then swaying back and forth. Once the benches were returned safely to the ground, the crowd stood and whistled. They only sat back down when the magician bowed for the third time.

Looking exhausted with sweat dripping down his face, the magician turned the front chair toward the crowd and sat down. The elf assistant who'd flirted with Blinkly earlier emerged from backstage.

"Before I continue to amaze you," the magician took a mug and rag from the assistant, "I'm sure all of you want to know a little bit about me." He guzzled his drink and wiped the sweat from his brow. "I am Herbit the Magnificent, the greatest magician in the world. Recently, I defeated a wicked band of ice trolls torturing and killing ice fairies near the . . ."

"Get on with the show!" a very wrinkly, very grumpy-looking dwarf hollered. Her scowl caused a tuft of silvery hair on her chin to poke out.

"Very well then," Herbit huffed. He pointed his staff at the old dwarf and yelled, "Andia—Molas—Afay!"

With the audience snickering, she floated through the air, flailing and shouting in protest. She was gently deposited into the chair next to Herbit.

"Thank you for volunteering," Herbit grinned. The crowd roared. She folded her arms and glared at him. "Now, I need two more volunteers," Herbit announced. "Who would like to perform some magic today?"

Half of the audience, including Nate, stood up and frantically waved their arms. "Me, me! Over here, pick me!"

"How about this pretty little thing?" Herbit pointed his staff at a woman with a petite nose and wavy, golden hair. Tapping a chair with his staff, Herbit said, "Azuba—Cram." She instantly appeared in the seat and shrilled with delight. Herbit again wiped the sweat from his forehead and scanned the crowd. Catching Nate's eye he smiled. "Come on up here, boy. It's your lucky day."

Leaping onto the stage, Nate did several cartwheels and a back flip—at least that's what he imagined—eagerly making his way to the empty seat at the back of the table. His body pulsed with excitement until Derik and his thugs started to chant. "Stut-ter-boy! Stut-ter-boy!" Nate's enthusiasm faded.

The chanting became louder. Herbit stood and yelled, "Silence!"

The crowd quieted, but Nate's stomach tangled in knots. He pulled at the neck of his shirt, trying to cool off. *What am I doing?* He slouched back into his chair and gazed out into the crowd.

"A staff," Herbit explained, "amplifies the caster's spell." The elf assistant reappeared and traded Herbit's staff for two wands. She returned backstage. "Wands cast specific spells. Anybody can use one if they know the magic words."

He held up a dark-blue wand. "This is the Wand of the Lake. It was given to me by a grateful merqueen because I saved her kingdom from an evil merwitch." He held up a crystal wand. "This one is the Wand of Freezing, a reward for saving the ice fairies, which I *tried* to mention earlier."

Taking her hand, Herbit helped the woman to her feet and declared, "This beautiful lady will be my first assistant."

Herbit handed her the Wand of the Lake, walked her over to the right side of the stage, and explained loudly, "When I tell you, point this wand at me and say 'Wat—Eran!'"

"What was that?" The lady asked, clearly nervous.

"Wat—Eran!" the crowd yelled excitedly.

Herbit walked briskly to the other side of the stage, spun around, and yelled, "Now!"

"Wat—Eran!" The lady timidly pointed the wand at Herbit. A powerful stream of water shot out of the wand.

Herbit calmly pointed the Wand of Freezing and said, "Frez—Eran!" A cloud of white smoke engulfed the stream of water, turning it to ice. The icicle hung momentarily in midair before crashing to the ground, breaking into thousands of tiny slivers.

The crowd stomped their feet and whistled. Several stage hands hurriedly swept up the shards of ice. The lady bowed proudly. Herbit took the wand and kissed her hand gently.

"Well done! Your talent matches your beauty." He helped her to the stairs. Returning to the center of the stage, he motioned for Nate and the dwarf to join him.

"Now for my next two volunteers." He handed the dark-blue wand to the grumpy dwarf. "This nice young lady," he announced with a wink to the chuckling crowd, "will have the Wand of the Lake. And this handsome young man," he handed the crystal wand to Nate, "will use the Wand of Freezing." After reminding them of the magic words, Herbit sent them to opposite sides of the stage. He stepped back toward the table, and yelled, "Begin!"

"Wat—Eran!" The dwarf yelled, swiftly pointing her wand at Nate, producing a powerful stream of water.

"F–F-Frez . . ." Nate stuttered nervously. Water hit him in the face, soaking his clothes.

The crowd erupted with laughter. Hanging his head in humiliation, Nate wanted to run. Derik and his entourage stood chanting, "Stut-ter-boy! Stut-ter-boy!" The crowd joined in. The chanting grew louder.

"Quiet! Quiet everyone!" Herbit shouted. The chanting stopped. Herbit hurried over to where Nate stood rigidly mortified. "Everyone deserves a second chance. We'll let him try again." In a low voice, Herbit spoke just to Nate, "Okay boy, you need to move much faster. Just relax." He gently rocked Nate's shoulders. "As soon as I say begin, point your wand at her and yell 'Frez—Eran.' Can you do that?"

"I th-th-think so." Nate jiggled the wand nervously.

Herbit walked back to the table shaking his head doubtfully. He turned toward the crowd, and yelled, "Begin!"

Nate flicked the wand but it shot out of his wet hand like an arrow from a bow. Just as the she yelled, "Wat—Eran," Nate's wand struck the old dwarf between the eyes. With a screech, she stumbled backward, spraying icy water on the crowd. She fell off the stage and landed on the ponytailed man. The drenched crowd turned their anger toward Nate.

One voice stood out. "Get him!"

In a daze, Nate turned just as the bullies pulled bags out from under their benches. He was pelted with rotten tomatoes.

He heard another distinct voice. "Nate!" From behind an open curtain flap, Blinkly yelled over the jeers of the crowd, "Nate, this way!"

Nate dashed toward him, nearly knocking down the elf assistant. He escaped out the back with Herbit cursing at them to never come back.

Chapter Six

A HIDEOUS CREATURE

Outside the tent, Nate and Blinkly muscled their way through a crowd of spectators who buzzed with questions. They ran until they reached the eating contests on the far side of the field.

"I was terrible!" Nate exclaimed.

"No worse than that magician," Blinkly countered. "Any wizard flunky could do those basic spells."

"At least he knows some magic," Nate grumbled. "I couldn't even use a wand." He pulled tomato chunks out of his hair and flung them to the ground. "I'll never be a wizard."

"You definitely won't with that attitude. Now, follow me," Blinkly motioned. "I need your help." He ran around the outskirts of the field, past the fortune teller's tent. When the draped cage came into view, Nate cringed and slowed down.

"Blinkly! Blinkly, stop!" Nate planted his feet. "What're you doing? I'm soaking wet and starving. Let's go home."

Blinkly stopped. "All I want to do is talk to it."

"What?"

"You'll see. Come on." Blinkly started toward the cage.

Nate followed reluctantly.

They rounded the cage. The curtain rested on an open back door. Tiptoeing closer, they peeked inside. To Nate's surprise, they spied a creature that acted nothing like the one they had seen earlier. Instead of growling and thrashing around ferociously, it sat on its hind legs, its wings tucked loosely behind its back. It lapped water out of three wooden buckets.

A crippled, yet muscular, young boy about Nate's age was inside the cage. Supported by a crudely carved, wooden crutch, his ebony skin matched his dreadlocked hair. His tattered shirt hung loosely over his cutoff denim pants and matched the ragged condition of his sandals. He spoke to the creature kindly, brushing tomatoes from its golden hair.

"I told you it wasn't vicious," Blinkly whispered.

"Maybe not with him, but it would probably eat *us*." Nate continued to watch in amazement.

Once the creature's fur was smooth and clean, the young man tossed the brush into an empty bucket and petted the neck of the wolf head.

"Good boy, you're a gooooood boy."

The bull head bumped the wolf head.

"Watch those horns, fella." The young man grabbed the bull's horns playfully.

The bear head growled softly.

"I haven't forgotten you." He scratched the bear head behind the ears. "That's all for now, I've got to feed the mules. See you after the next show."

Shrugging off the wolf head's attempt to lick him, the young man balanced the buckets on one arm. He limped toward the back door. Nate and Blinkly darted around the side.

When they heard the cage door close, Blinkly whispered, "I'm going to talk to him."

"Just don't get eaten," Nate said.

"Not the creature!" Blinkly jogged after the hobbling young man. Nate followed. "Excuse me, sir." Blinkly easily caught him.

The young man stopped.

"Hi, I'm Blinkly. This is my friend, Nate." Blinkly nodded over his shoulder.

"I'm Zeldon, what can I do for you?" He cradled his crutch under his left arm.

"My friend thinks that creature is vicious. It didn't hurt you did it?" Blinkly asked.

"No way, not Demon."

"Demon?" Nate raised his eyebrows.

"He was named Demon so he'd sound dangerous," Zeldon explained. "It doesn't fit him at all."

"But we saw the way he acted." Nate gestured to the cage.

"You'd act that way, too, if you were prodded with a hot iron before a show," Zeldon explained with contempt.

"I see." Nate regretted his assumption. "Why don't you let him go then?"

"Yeah, how can you stand to watch him being tormented?"

"I never watch the show." Zeldon adjusted his weight on his crutch. "I'd free Demon if I could, but my mother and I would be kicked out of the festival. We'd have nowhere to go."

"What if I bought him?" Blinkly asked.

"Not likely. Demon is the Trapper's prize catch." Zeldon motioned with his head to a tent on the slope behind the cage.

"That fool selling the rotten tomatoes?" Blinkly asked.

"That's him." Zeldon looked disgusted. "He makes a killing at every show."

"There has to be something we can do for Demon," Blinkly muttered.

"I really wish I could help." Zeldon suddenly seemed nervous. "I've got to get the cage key back to the Trapper. He's waiting on me so he can take his nap. He gets awful cross if he has to wait."

"Sorry to keep you so long," Blinkly said.

Zeldon hobbled toward the Trapper's tent.

Nate and Blinkly took a few steps in silence.

"I've got it!" Blinkly snapped his fingers. "Come on." Blinkly led Nate behind the cage. "When the Trapper falls asleep, I'm going to free Demon."

Nate gaped at Blinkly.

"Don't worry, Nate." Blinkly peeked around the cage. "I'll blink in and grab the key before he even knows I was there."

"I'm not going to talk you out of it, am I?"

Blinkly shook his head.

Rolling his eyes, Nate sat down next to the cage. A rustle sounded behind the curtain. Blinkly raised it slightly. He was face-to-face with Demon. The bear head growled, the wolf head snarled, and the bull head snorted. Nate scrambled away from the cage. Blinkly remained motionless, muttering something under his breath. The growling, snarling, and snorting got louder.

"What are you doing?" Nate demanded.

"Talking to him." Blinkly remained calm, his eyes locked with the wolf's eyes. He muttered again.

Demon quieted. The bull tilted and stared. The bear whimpered. The wolf licked Blinkly's face through the cage.

Nate inched forward. Rising to his feet, he stretched his hand through the cage bars. He gently rubbed the bear head.

The bear nuzzled his snout into Nate's palm.

"Unbelievable!" Nate scratched the bear's neck. He wanted to take Demon home.

"We're going to get you out of here." Blinkly patted the bull. "Let's go, Nate."

They replaced the curtain. Glancing around, they hustled to the tent flap. They heard deep breathing. Blinkly peeked inside.

"The key's too high for me to reach and there's nothing I can blink onto," Blinkly whispered. "Will you get it?"

Nate peered inside the tent. There was no doubt the snoring man inside was a trapper. A long-handled silver axe leaned against a mound of iron traps. Colorful animal pelts hung from the tent's support beams. Another corner boasted a large, open chest of fur clothing. The Trapper slept on a thick, dark-red bear rug in the middle of the tent. His double-edged knife lay within his reach. Dangling directly above his head on a rack of silver antlers secured to the center post, hung the key to Demon's cage.

Rubbing his forearm, Nate winced. The painful memory of being pelted with rotten tomatoes was fresh on his mind. He crept through the flap, accidently kicking a pebble. It rolled several times before knocking against an iron trap. Nate froze in place, his heart beating wildly.

Mumbling, the Trapper rolled onto his side. He started to snore again.

Nate rushed to the key. He didn't lift it high enough and it caught on the tip of the antlers.

When he pulled the key away, the antlers banged loudly against the post.

"Who's there?" the Trapper sat up, his knife already in his hand. Grasping the key tightly in his fist, Nate kicked the center post and dove for the exit. The tent collapsed onto the Trapper.

"Quick thinking." Blinkly took the key and blinked his way to the cage. Nate sprinted closely behind him.

Blinkly swung the cage door open. They rushed inside. Demon bounded toward them, licking Blinkly's face.

"Come on, boy," Blinkly coaxed. Petting Demon, he led him out the door.

From up the hill, the Trapper's gravelly voice yelled, "Stop!"

Demon's heads snapped up. He began cowering back into his cage. The Trapper charged toward them.

"Fly! Fly!" Nate flapped his arms. Blinkly stroked the side of the bear's head, whispering into his ear.

Demon stepped past Blinkly away from the cage and spread his massive wings. A few mighty flaps raised him high in the air out of the Trapper's reach.

"You'll pay for that!" The Trapper sprinted with effort toward them.

"Into the cage!" Blinkly ordered.

"Are you crazy?"

"Trust me." Blinkly ran into the cage. Nate hesitated only long enough to see the fury in the Trapper's eyes. He joined Blinkly inside at the front of the cage.

"Quick, slide through the bars."

Nate struggled through the bars. For once, he was glad he was skinny. He searched for an opening in the curtain. Blinkly still stood inside the cage.

"What are you waiting for?" Nate asked in disbelief. The Trapper reached the back door.

"You want me?" Blinkly goaded the Trapper. "Come get me!"

In a rage, the Trapper charged. Just as the Trapper reached him, Blinkly disappeared, reappearing outside the back door. The Trapper crashed into the cage bars. He could have grabbed Nate if he hadn't knocked himself down in a daze. Slamming the cage closed, Blinkly locked the door. He threw the key far into the open field.

"Let's see how you like being a caged animal!" Blinkly yelled.

Blinkly ran around the side of the cage. Nate dropped to his belly and rolled under the bottom of the curtain. They rushed to the outskirts of the field with the Trapper's screams fading behind them.

"We'd better split up," Nate suggested. "The Trapper should leave with the festival tomorrow."

Nate rushed home to help prepare dinner. He told his family Banner Day was uneventful. He pretended to be interested in Ted's day and allowed him to do all the talking. Nate made an excuse to go to bed before the red moon entered the sky.

"Wake up, Nate!" Nate's brother shook him from a deep sleep. "It's payback time."

Nate groggily opened his eyes. He could barely make out Ted's silhouette standing over him.

Chapter Seven

PAYBACK

"**P**ayback for what?" Nate grumpily shook the heaviness from his eyelids.

"For savin' ya from Derik. Get yer clothes on," Ted ordered.

Oh yeah, Nate grinned. Still sleepy, he was less annoyed and dressed quickly. Following Ted into the front hall, the sound of someone sawing a tree in half drifted from his parents' bedroom door, confirming their mother was sleeping soundly. His father's skinny, white legs hung off the end of the hay bed. Nate crept behind Ted to the front door.

Ted handed Nate an iron lantern and flung a crossbow over his shoulder. He slid the door's iron bolt to the side. They slipped out. Nate pulled the door behind them. It squeaked shut. He cringed.

The purple moon was setting behind the forest. The orange moon rose in the sky. Nate followed Ted down the front steps. "It's the middle of the night!"

"Really?" Ted's reply dripped with sarcasm. He broke into a sprint.

Nate chased Ted between their father's work shed and the outhouse toward the trail leading west to Gemstone Mountain. It was one of the tallest mountains in Versii. At the head of the trail, Ted stopped suddenly and spun around.

Jumping aside to avoid a collision, Nate skidded to a stop. "What're you doing?"

"Give me the lantern." Ted pulled some flint out of his pocket and knelt down.

Thrusting the lantern to Ted, Nate shivered. The Darkoak Forest, named for the thousands of bulky, towering trees that dominated the landscape, surrounded them. The swaying tree branches danced like devilish creatures. After lighting the candle, Ted stood up. The forest was illuminated and the ominous villains vanished. They continued their journey at a brisk pace.

"When are you going to tell me what we're doing?" Nate asked.

"After ya tell me about yer trouble at the festival."

"What do you mean?"

"Throwin' a wand at old Mrs. Goobler! Soakin' the townsfolk at the magic show! Freein' a vicious monster!" Ted snapped.

Nate's jaw dropped. "H-h-how'd you know about all that?"

"I've got my spies."

"No really, tell me! Then I'll fill you in on what really happened," Nate insisted.

"Well . . . all right. Nordof and I were passin' the magic show when we heard a lot of screamin'. We snuck inside just as ya ran behind the stage curtain. Nordof's sister, who ya drenched, ran over ta us and said ya were mad at Old Mrs. Goobler cuz she got ya wet so ya threw yer wand at her and knocked her off the stage."

"That's not true! It was an accident," Nate proclaimed his innocence. "I never meant to hit her. The wand just slipped out of my hand."

"That's not what everyone else is sayin'. Besides, even if it was an accident, ya still humiliated her. I heard she went straight ta her son, Captain Goobler, and now he's lookin' for ya."

"That would be my luck. Of all the old dwarfs to hit . . ."

"Well, at least that crazy Trapper is gone."

"What do you mean?"

"After leavin' the magic show, which ended early thanks ta yer prank, this crazy guy grabbed my arm and threatened ta kill me for lettin' his creature go. I yanked my arm away and told him if he touched me again I'd break his nose. He pulled out this huge double-edged knife. We were about ta run when he demanded ta know if I had a brother that hung out with a short elf fella."

"What did you tell him?"

"After what ya did ta Mrs. Goobler I wasn't claimin' ya as my brother anymore so I said no. He stormed off mutterin' something under his breath. We saw him leave in his wagon. The kid who hitched it up told us he'd gone ta track that creature and wouldn't rest until he caught it again."

"Well, I hope he never catches him. Demon doesn't deserve to be caged." Nate tightened his lips.

"So ya *did* free his monster!" Ted accused.

"Yeah, but he's not a monster!"

"That thing's vicious. You just called it a demon."

"He's not a demon. His *name* is Demon."

"Demon or not, he wasn't yers ta free. I really worry about ya Nate, ya need ta be more responsible." Ted held the lantern in front of him while they jogged down the path.

Nate's mind raced furiously. *Responsible! How's running through the woods in the middle of the night responsible? Besides, he's the king of mischief. Who does he think he is to lecture me?* It didn't take long for Nate's thoughts to drift to his own problems. He was relieved the Trapper had left town but feared his punishment when Captain Goobler found him. They wound along the twisty trail. Nate wondered if they would ever stop. Ted slowed to a walk.

"This is ridiculous," Nate protested. "What are we doing?"

"Follow me and ya'll see." Ted blew the candle out and set the lantern down. "Not a sound!"

Stepping off the trail, Ted tiptoed through the brush and fallen branches. Nate struggled to follow quietly. He could barely see anything in the orange moonlight.

Suddenly, a terrifying screech pierced the silence. Nate spun around. An owl snatched a hairy rodent off the ground behind him. His heart pounded. Nate threw his arms over his head and ducked. The owl barely missed him as it flew into the night sky. To Nate's surprise, Ted, several strides ahead of him, acted as if nothing had happened.

Nate realized his eyes had adjusted to the darkness. He shook off the panic that had briefly gripped him. He rushed to catch up. A thicket of brush blocked their path. Ted followed the lofty bushes, dropped to his knees, and disappeared.

Now where'd he go? Nate wasn't amused. He took several steps along the thicket. Dropping to his knees, he searched until he noticed a narrow opening. Struggling through the thorny brush, he scraped his head several times. The further he crawled, the more frustrated he became. The dirt turned into mud. The sound of rushing water grew louder. They were nearing Greatfalls River.

He's crazy if he thinks I'm going swimming in the middle of the night! Nate's frustration with Ted was peaking.

Ted stopped. He waved to Nate. Squeezing up next to Ted at the edge of the thicket, Nate rested his arms on the muddy embankment. They overlooked dark, rushing water.

"Over there," Ted whispered, pointing to the opposite side of the river. A herd of wild pegasi drank along the water's edge. "I've been watchin' them for a while now. The black one is their leader."

Nate's frustration turned to bewilderment.

Alert and on guard, the pegasus leader scanned the forest. Nearby, several pegasi drank from the river. A short distance away, a baby pegasus playfully flitted along the embankment.

"Tonight, ya're goin' ta help me fly."

"This is your idea of being *responsible*?" Nate worked hard to keep his voice low.

"I said *you* hafta be responsible, I didn't say nothin' about me. I can't become the champion if I don't win. I can't win if I've never ridden a pegasus! Now follow me." Ted crawled backward.

Nate worked his way back through the thicket. Keeping his head down, he avoided the thorns. When he exited, he raised his head a moment too soon. A thorn sank deep into his forehead. He bit his tongue to stifle a scream. He turned to snap at Ted. Two glowing red eyes charged toward him.

Blood rats came out at night and were drawn to the slightest smell of blood. From the oozing he felt on his forehead, Nate knew he was in trouble.

The five-boot long, furless, pink rodent charged, snarling ferociously. Its fang-like teeth glistened in the moonlight.

Tense from head to toe, Nate eyed a nearby tree, ready to make a run for it. He heard the distinct ping of a crossbow. Struck deep in its side by the bolt, the blood rat let out an eerie yelp, took another step toward Nate, and fell lifelessly to the ground. A rustle to his left caused Nate to jump. Ted rushed toward him.

"Stop the bleedin' with this." Ted handed Nate a yumber leaf. "Unless ya want more blood rats ta find ya."

Nate quickly covered the wound.

"Let's get movin'." Ted reshouldered the crossbow. Leading Nate to a towering jagged cliff at the end of the thicket, his brother hardly paused before beginning his climb. He was halfway to the top before Nate had even started.

Nate searched the rocks and bushes for natural footholds and slowly scaled the cliff. The ever increasing roar of rushing water made him anxious. He cleared the thicket. Orange moonlight reflected off the gushing waterfall

about twenty boot-lengths away. He wished
desperately he was home asleep, not plodding
after his reckless brother. At the top of the cliff,
Ted waited at the edge of the falls. A fallen
darkoak tree created a natural bridge to the other
side.

"We're not going across that, are we?" Nate
eyed the silhouettes of jagged rocks below.

"Unless ya'd rather go back down and swim
across," Ted grinned. "Come on. We haven't got
all night."

Ted moved between the branches with
impressive speed and agility. He leapt safely onto
the opposite bank. Nate took a deep breath and
stepped onto the fallen tree bridge. Gripping each
limb as if his life depended on it, he started
across. Watching his footing and trying to ignore
the raging falls below, he finally reached the other
side.

"It's about time." Ted yanked him off the tree
by his shirt. "How a coward like ya ever expects ta
be a wizard I don't know."

"Well at least I'm educated! You'd be, too, if
you cared about what mother tries to teach us."

"I don't need education ta be a champion but if ya don't find some courage ya'll never amount ta nothing." Ted started down the cliff. "Now hurry!"

Nate clambered behind Ted. He made it to the river's edge. "Now what?"

"They're around that corner." Ted pointed ahead of them. "Unless they're gone cuz ya were too slow!"

"You're the one who told me to be more responsible!"

"Not tonight! Now shut up and listen. When I leave, start countin'." Ted grinned. He spoke fast and waved his arms. "At five hundred, run along the river screamin' as loud as ya can ta scare the pegasuses. I'll be in a tree and will jump onta one of them before they take off."

"If you're not back in two days, I'm taking your stuff," Nate whispered.

"Ya better give me a week." Ted handed Nate the crossbow. "One more thing, if ya don't scare them, they'll kick your teeth out." He darted into the trees out of sight.

One, two, three . . . four hundred ninety-nine, five hundred, Nate counted in his head. *Here goes nothing.*

Nate walked to the river's edge. He braced himself and started screaming at the top of his lungs. He hoped the pegasi would already be on the run before they spotted him. He rounded the corner. To his relief, the startled pegasi were bolting down the embankment away from him. They didn't even look back. He stomped wildly along the water's edge.

The herd neared a clearing. Ted was perched on a branch overhanging the embankment. He leaped onto the back of a light-colored pegasus. Hooking his feet behind the wings, he grasped the tail, holding on tightly. The pegasus bucked twice before running after the others. Bounding into the air, the pegasus beat its majestic wings gracefully and rose higher into the sky. Nate watched in awe as the flying herd disappeared over the forest taking Ted with them!

Chapter Eight

THE WHITE CASTLE

Nate's journey back home was uneventful. No screeching owl, snarling blood rat, or bossy brother pressuring him to rush across a death-defying waterfall. His only challenge was the time it took to find where they'd left the old lantern. He reached the edge of the forest. The mid-day sun shone brightly.

Passing the work shed, Nate racked his brain. *What'll I tell mother and father if Ted's not back for dinner?* He rounded the corner. His mother was talking to Mrs. Goobler and her son. Captain Goobler had a full beard that reached the top of his breastplate and a rough battle-scarred face. Jumping back, Nate peered around the corner.

"Mrs. Goobler, I'm so very sorry for what my son did to you. I promise he'll make amends," his mother assured.

"He'd better," Mrs. Goobler grumbled. Captain Goobler helped her down the steps.

"If he doesn't, he'll have to answer to me." Captain Goobler helped Mrs. Goobler into their buggy. He heaved himself up on the other side. "Good day." He snapped the reins. The stallion trotted away.

Nate paced next to the barn several times before he worked up the courage to face his mother. He walked heavily up the front steps, pushed open their squeaky door, and stepped inside. Setting the lantern down, he closed the door.

74

His mother burst in from the kitchen. "Nathanial McGray! Where've you been?" She wiped her hands on her apron. Standing nearly five boot-lengths tall, she had a broad frame. Her rough, wrinkled skin reflected years of hard work.

"H-h-helping Ted train for the tryouts." Nate slid the crossbow off his shoulder, leaning it next to the lantern.

"I just had a very embarrassing visit because of you."

"Oh, really?" Nate played innocent.

"I can't believe what you did to Mrs. Goobler! I'd expect something like this from Ted, not you." His mother rubbed the back of her neck.

"It was an a-a-accident! My hands were wet. The wand just slipped out. I didn't do it on purpose!"

"Accident or not, you'll have to make amends." His mother crossed her arms over her chest.

"B-b-but . . ."

"No buts." His mother cut him off. "Mrs. Goobler recently moved here from the Golden Mountains. She bought one of the halfling burrows. It needs some fixing up and you're going to help."

"A burrow? Her son's one of the king's captains. Why would she want to live in an old burrow?"

"I didn't see the need to ask. You're starting tomorrow."

Suddenly, the door swung open. It slammed into Nate.

"Ow!" He jumped out of the way.

"Sorry about that." Nate's father stepped into the house. "Ya shouldn't be standin' in the doorway."

"You'll never believe the trouble Nathanial has been causing." They all moved into the kitchen. His mother proceeded to tell his father about Mrs. Goobler.

"Ya're lucky she wasn't seriously injured. Things could have been much worse." His father took two bowls from his mother.

"I know." *I don't agree but they won't care.* Nate sat down at their kitchen table.

"Better eat fast." His father started on his lunch of bland squirrel stew. "We're headin' ta the castle when we're done." Nate's hope for a nap disappeared. "A drunk Count fell off a balcony last night. He left a hole in the woodshed roof and a storm's rollin' in. That wood'll be soaked if we don't get it patched."

"Can't someone else help?"

"I'm the woodsman, Nathanial. It's my job. Ya're goin' ta help."

Nate slumped in his chair and finished his lunch.

When Nate and his father started for the castle, rolling dark clouds in the distance blocked out the sun. By the time the wagon reached Main Street, a stiff breeze ruffled Nate's hair. As always, the cobblestone walkway bustled with townsfolk. Some stopped to socialize but most hurried in and out of the different shops seemingly unfazed by the approaching storm.

The last store along Main Street was Nate's favorite. Gillard's Magic Shop was guarded by Bilerd and Bowe, two cyclops brothers who carried massive spiked clubs. They were not friendly. Following the orders of Gillard Duberry, the bad-tempered halfling who owned the magic shop, they turned away any townsfolk who couldn't afford to buy. Nate gawked through the window regularly but had never been inside.

"Whoa!" Nate's father cried, pulling back on the reins. He stopped just short of two messy-haired boys who darted into the middle of the road. Caught up in a daydream about the magic shop, Nate toppled off the wagon and landed head first in a steaming pile of fresh horse manure.

"Blaah!" Nate spat, sitting up. He flicked nasty green dung off his hands. "I got to go home."

His father chuckled. "Sorry, but we don't have time. Clean yourself up over there." He motioned to a trough in front of the magic shop.

With a glance at the rapidly approaching storm clouds, Nate plodded over to the trough. Bowe was laughing hysterically, his big eye filling with tears. Bilerd was as emotionless as ever.

I don't think it's funny, either. Nate dunked his upper body into the water. It removed the dung, but the foul stench remained. He climbed back into the wagon.

"This won't take long," his father reassured.

Nate sulked in his seat.

They started up the hill. The White Castle rose regally above them. A band of cavalry riders wearing light chain mail armor and open-faced helmets galloped past them. Nate's spirits lifted slightly.

"They're sure in a hurry." Nate imagined they were off to fight a giant two-headed troll, a gang of ruthless bandits, or pirates attacking the Crimson City.

"They've been trainin' a lot," his father said.

Within the castle's enormous bronze gates, the outer courtyard was abuzz with activity. At the barracks, knights engaged in mock sword fights. Archers lined the range, taking aim at a row of targets. Dwarfs tested a spinner—a massive wheel that fired hundreds of icy spikes. Heavy grey smoke billowed out of all five of the tall armory chimneys. Nate had never seen more than two in use at one time.

"Why's everyone working so hard?" Nate asked.

"There's talk about a wicked king who's declared war against Zndaria. It's just rumors, but the army's preparin' just in case."

Flooded with memories from the mural in Blinkly's room, Nate's stomach lurched. "What if the rumors are true?"

"Ya don't need ta worry about that," his father insisted. "If it is true, King Darwin will protect us."

The wagon passed through the inner wall. Lightning streaked across the sky. Before Nate could count to five, a loud clap of thunder startled the mules.

"Easy boys." Nate's father pulled on the reins. He guided the mules to the woodshed on the far side of the Keep—a ten-story structure that housed the royal family and advisors.

Nate's father secured the wagon. Nate hopped out and grabbed the wood planks and nails. Racing against the impending storm, Nate and his father repaired the hole. Nate drove the last nail. A raindrop fell on his cheek. They ducked inside the shed. A light shower danced on the roof.

"Looks good," his father approved. "Take care of the mules while I make my rounds. Ya can wait for me at the stables."

"When the rain stops, I'm out of here." Nate gestured with renewed frustration at his soiled clothing.

Nate dashed to the wagon and drove the mules across the deserted inner courtyard. He reached the royal stables. The sky opened up and the drizzle became a downpour. After securing the mules, Nate slid the first door closed. A bolt of lightning illuminated the sky. Nate stopped. The Red Wizard's tower loomed above the Keep, blanketed by black rain clouds. The gloomy dark redstone tower tapered from its base to the Wizard's living quarters high at the top.

How a coward like ya ever expects ta be a wizard I don't know. Ted's words haunted Nate. He stared at the Red Wizard's closed shutters. Thunder clapped. Nate bolted out of the stable. Sloshing through the mud, he reached the tower in several long strides. Dripping wet, he pulled open the heavy door. He stepped inside and it slammed shut behind him—engulfing him in utter darkness.

Chapter Nine

THE INCREDIBLY TALL TOWER

Immediately questioning his sanity, a wave of fear washed over Nate. Spinning around, his hands searched the cold, iron door for an escape. His shadow suddenly appeared on the door. His hands froze. Heat blazed on the back of his neck.

Inhaling sharply, he turned around. Flaming
words hovered in midair.

**Do not pass through the doors within
unless you possess self-discipline.
You must overcome that which is sin
or fail you will, time and time again.**

Nate read the warning a second time. The fiery
words merged into a fireball, brightly illuminating
his surroundings. Appearing uninviting, the
tower's base was void of any furnishings. Dark
redstone stairs spiraled steeply upward,
disappearing into the blackness above.

The blazing sphere drifted toward the stairs.
Nate glanced over his shoulder. *How'd I miss
that?* There was a distinct iron latch on the door.
Determined to run, he reached for the latch. He
hesitated. *No wonder Ted thinks I'm a coward. If I
don't do this, I'll never have a chance of becoming
a wizard.*

Squaring his shoulders, Nate spun around.
With lengthy strides, he reached the stairs. He
rushed up them two at a time until he caught up

to the fireball. The bottom of the tower was swallowed in darkness. A sharp drop-off awaited him on either side. Cautiously keeping to the center, he pondered the fiery riddle.

'Do not pass through the doors within', Nate thought of the door he'd left below. *Too late for that. 'Unless you possess self-discipline.' I don't get into near as much trouble as Ted.* Rounding a turn, the stairs ended in front of a luminous orange door. The fiery guide vanished. Nate approached warily. The smooth door swung open. Bright orange light spilled out.

Nate recalled the rest of the warning, *'You must overcome that which is sin or fail you will, time and time again.'* He mustered his courage and took two giant steps into the center of the empty room. The door slammed shut. He flinched and glanced from the high ceiling to the whitewashed walls. All radiated an orange glow. He heard loud fluttering overhead.

Peering upward again, Nate marveled. A pedestal table with petite, dark orange wings gracefully swooped around above the room. Landing delicately, the table began to quake, rattling against the stone floor. The sound of splitting wood replaced the quaking. The pedestal base divided cleanly into four legs. They wiggled briefly and took several hops apart. The table expanded to triple its size, striking Nate in the thighs. He stumbled backward.

A dark-orange chair with a high back and armrests appeared. It strutted over and scooped Nate up in its seat. It marched him to the head of the table. The room filled with the intoxicating aroma of chocolateberries. Nate gaped as bowls of chocolateberry pudding, several chocolateberry pies, plates of chocolateberry bread, a towering chocolateberry cake, and goblets full of chocolateberry cider floated down. The table was completely covered.

Overwhelmed by the tempting scent, Nate debated which treat to taste first. *This must be heaven,* Nate marveled. Grabbing a spoon, he dug into a chocolateberry pie. He savored the fudgy cream that melted in his mouth. He went for a second bite, but his thumb jiggled, wiggled, and popped to twice its normal size!

"Whoa!" Nate jumped up, flinging the spoon into a bowl of pudding. It splattered everywhere. Picturing Thorton spread on three infirmary beds, he patted the rest of his body. Everything else appeared normal.

The chair slammed into the back of his legs. He fell into the seat. The chair spun around on one leg. The door opened. The chair marched toward it. Nate watched in alarm. With a thunderous grating sound, the stairs transformed into a slick, stone slide. *I'm not getting thrown out!* The chair reached the exit. Nate kicked the doorframe, throwing his weight against the back of the chair. He and the chair tumbled over.

Struggling to his feet, Nate noticed a second door on the opposite side of the room. The table rammed into his legs, forcing him toward the slide. He clambered onto it and scurried across. Chocolateberry goodies flew everywhere. Leaping to the ground, he lunged for the door. He grasped the iron latch, pushed his way out, and slammed the door shut.

What just happened? Nate breathed deeply to slow his racing heart. The fireball reappeared.

The spiraling staircase started again. *This will all be worth it if I can just talk to the Red Wizard.* He climbed countless stairs until the flaming orb left him at a glowing yellow door.

"Here goes nothing," Nate muttered to himself. He stepped inside the dazzling golden room.

The door slammed shut. Thousands of gold coins plinked down on top of him, as if from a spout in the ceiling. Nate shielded his head with his arms until the downpour ceased. He'd seen a gold bit one time when Thorton bragged about his family's wealth. Mesmerized, he squinted from the glare reflecting off the mounds surrounding him. Nate was buried up to his knees in gold!

A smile stole across Nate's face. *My favorite wand at Gillard's Magic Shop costs one gold bit! There's so much here, one bit won't be missed!* He pulled his legs out of the mound, plucked a gold bit off the pile, and slipped it into his pocket.

A new door appeared across the room. Nate scrambled over the heaps of gold. Releasing the door latch, he was startled by the sound of thousands of eggs cracking all at once. He backed out the door, horrified to see that the gold bits had split open, hatching a throng of hairy, long-legged spiders.

Several spiders sprang toward him. "Ugggh!" He slammed the door against muted thuds. He jumped back to avoid yellow goo splattering on the landing. Four hairy legs protruded from the door frame. A squirming in his pocket sent an icy chill down his back.

A hideous spider wriggled out of his pocket. Nate panicked. Slapping wildly with his overgrown thumb, he knocked the spider to the ground. It shot a yellow web onto Nate's pant leg. Nate stomped on the spider. Yellow slime oozed from underneath his boot. He twisted his foot several times to make sure the spider was dead.

I can't touch anything. Nate felt flustered knowing that his mother had taught him better. He followed the fireball. It disappeared and he paused. *Touch nothing!* He reminded himself before entering a radiant sapphire-blue room.

The door closed quietly. The wall in front of him split down the middle, revealing an all-white chamber. A tapestry carpet covered the floor. Small tables displayed dozens of fresh roses in crystal vases. A silky canopy hanging from the four-post bed fluttered like angel wings.

Seated at the foot of the bed, her arms resting in her lap, was the most stunning woman Nate had ever seen. Her white gown dipped slightly at the neck, hugged her slender waist, and flowed elegantly to her ankles. Her red hair cascaded down her back. Piercing blue eyes stared playfully at Nate. Her crimson lips smiled. Captivated by her beauty, Nate stood rooted to the floor.

She glided toward him, her hips swaying as she moved. She took his hand, intertwining their fingers. "Come with me." She pulled Nate toward the bed.

Nate took several steps before shaking his head to wake himself from what felt like an incredible dream. He pulled his hand from hers.

"I c-c-can't do this." Nate backed away.

"Of course you can." The woman's melodious voice whispered in his ear. "No one will ever know."

Nate spied the exit door and started toward it in a brisk walk.

A bloodcurdling shriek sounded behind him. "You can't leave me!"

Glancing back, Nate saw the once-stunning woman was now a hideous hag floating several boot-lengths in the air. Her slender body had shriveled. Her flowing hair was a mass of unruly tangles. Her perfect skin had wrinkled and was spotted with fat, hairy moles.

Grimacing, Nate stumbled backward and pushed the door open. The hag swooped in, grabbed him by the wrist, and pulled him back into the room. Her touch burned. Nate yanked his arm away, darted past the door, and threw it shut.

Annoyed by the hag's muffled screeching, Nate examined his wrist. *Ugh! And don't get touched!* It dripped with gooey blue slime. He flicked his wrist and the goo splattered on the landing. It left a dark-blue ring on his skin that reeked of curdled goat's milk.

The light was dwindling. Nate jerked his head up in time to see the fireball round a turn. Ready to distance himself from the nasty hag, he dashed up the stairs. He almost reached the orb when it vanished in front of a sparkling, emerald-green door. He didn't slow down. The door opened and he slid past, skidding to a stop inside the empty room.

As soon as the door closed, a green light flashed. Nate squeezed his eyes shut. When he opened them, he gawked. Hundreds—if not thousands—of wands hovered as if protruding from the wall in front of him.

"Whooooooooa!" Nate marveled at more wands than he could ever imagine. Their many bright colors made his head spin. One wand was long and dark purple, another was short and transparent, filled with a sparkling light-pink liquid. One shimmered silver and another appeared to be of the purest white.

The more wands he examined, the more his resentment grew. *I'd be happy to have any one of these wands. There's more here than anyone could ever use.* He reached the center of the wall. Directly in front of him were three crystal wands filled with glowing yellow liquid—his favorite wand at Gillard's. His footsteps froze.

"*Three!*" Nate bellowed, "I'd give anything for just one of those wands!"

Nate shot his arm up to take one of the wands. He spotted his oversized thumb and remembered the room with the chocolateberry treats.

I'm in the Red Wizard's tower! Nate felt a knot form in his stomach. *What am I doing?* Anxiety replaced his envy.

The wand he'd tried to grab mutated into a pale hand. It stretched toward him. Ducking away, Nate bolted. Every wand mutated and sprang to grab him. The further he moved away from the wall, the further the arms stretched, forcing him to stoop, jump, or slap them away.

He reached the exit and threw open the door. A hand caught him by the ear. Jerking free, his head slammed into the door frame. He tumbled into the hallway. Before he could pick himself up, another mutated wand grabbed his leg. Nate kicked the door shut with his free leg, severing the outstretched arm. Flashing as it hit the ground, the detached arm changed back into the tip of a pink crystal wand.

Nate stood and gingerly touched his goose egg. *Is this all worth it?* He shook his head gently. The fireball started up the stairs. He glanced around. *What if I just go back? At least I know what's in these rooms.* He reached for the door. The light faded around him. *Even if I could go back, I couldn't see going down the stairs. One wrong step and I'm dead.*

He didn't have a choice. He caught up with the fireball and plodded up the stairs. His legs burned. His feet ached. The fireball vanished in front of a glossy light-blue door. Nate sighed with frustration. Before the door had fully opened, he slipped inside.

An elegant chandelier emitted a soft blue light over a mahogany lounge chair. Four tapered legs elevated the base of the chair. A fluffy cushion covered the entire frame. The strings of a grand harp moved gently as if played by delicate, unseen hands, delivering tranquil, hypnotizing music.

Finally! A chance to rest, Nate thought. He strolled over to the chair and sunk into the soft cushion. He hadn't slept much the night before and surviving the tower rooms had worn him down. The chair fully reclined itself. He stretched out. *A short rest will do me some good.* Nate shut his eyes and relaxed to the continuous strumming of the harp.

In his dream, Nate soared through a majestic forest without wings. He glided over a sparkling lake, gently running his fingers across the water. He flew higher into the air and found himself flying next to Ted who still held onto the tail of the pegasus. Nate waved excitedly but then thought, *Ted? Flying? Wait—where am I?*

Nate jerked his eyes opened. His face was only a boot-length away from the ceiling. The chair tilted sharply and started down. Gripping the sides of the chair, Nate watched in horror. The chair rapidly approached an open window forming in the wall. He didn't want to leave like this. Bracing himself, he leaped off the chair. He hit the floor hard, sharply twisting his ankle. The chair flew out of the tower.

Wincing with each step, Nate reached the exit. *Razzle! I can't believe I fell asleep!* He staggered out the door. *I want to see the Red Wizard!* He limped up more stairs. The fireball disappeared in front of a blood-red door. Nate hobbled inside. Enormous mirrors covered the walls. He was surrounded by his reflection.

"I'm a mess!" Nate declared. His pants were caked with chocolateberry pie, yellow spider web, and blue slime. His wrist was dark blue; his right thumb was several times its normal size. A goose egg marred his forehead. His twisted ankle made him bend over like an old man. Inhaling, he gagged. He reeked of curdled goat's milk and horse manure.

All of a sudden, Nate's father appeared next to Nate's reflection.

"Look at yerself," his father chided. "I told ya it was foolish ta think ya could become a wizard. It's bad enough that Ted wants ta be a champion, but a wizard? Ridiculous. Impossible."

In the next instant, Marnia stood next to Nate's father and taunted, "You may think you're going to be a great wizard someday—but you're not! You're a poor nobody. That's all you'll ever be."

"You become a wizard?" Thorton appeared next to Marnia. "That's the stupidest thing I've ever heard. You're crazy!"

Growing louder, their repeating voices overlapped. Staring at his beat-up body and the unending reflections of his hecklers, Nate turned in circles. His heart pounded, his body tensed.

Images of Derik's goons appeared, adding their insults. Nate clenched his fists and tightened his jaw. Suddenly Derik appeared. "You'll never be a wizard. All you'll ever be is a stuttering punkler nickler!"

"You're w-w-wrong, you're a-a-all wrong!" Nate lunged at the mirror, striking Derik's image hard with both fists. A crack ringed around Nate's hands. Derik's image disappeared. Expanding from the circle, fractures riddled the rest of the mirrors, driving the other images away. Frigid water surged through the cracks. Nate gasped. The mirrors appeared to melt.

A melted mirror revealed another red door. Nate sloshed through the rising water. It rose to his chest by the time he reached the door. He heard a loud boom behind him. His stomach lurched. He looked over his shoulder. A whirlpool forming in the center of the room pulled at him.

Nate clutched the door handle. The current lifted him off the floor, drawing him powerfully toward the vortex. He gripped the handle with all his might, determined to stay in the tower. His body floated in the current. The pool roared out of the room. When all the water drained, Nate's feet returned to the floor. A trapdoor banged shut. He shuddered in relief.

His hand still tightly around the handle, Nate opened the door. He entered a fancy parlor. Dozens of crystal shelves displayed vases of violet lilies. An enormous chandelier sparkled. Nate's attention fixated on the person seated on the shimmering, golden throne in the center of the spacious room—a stern-faced Red Wizard.

Chapter Ten

THE RED WIZARD

Nate had seen the Red Wizard two other times in his life. When Nate was twelve years old, the Red Wizard led a band of cavalry riders past his home. Then last year, when Nate helped deliver a load of wood, the Red Wizard and King Darwin greeted a queen centaur on the steps of the castle Keep.

The Red Wizard seated in front of Nate imparted an aura of power. His muscular frame was cloaked in a scarlet robe that draped to the floor, covering his feet. Straight, red hair framed his stern face. His pointed beard hung over his lap. With his arms resting firmly on padded armrests, he held a golden staff with a massive purple gem affixed to the top.

Rising from his chair, the Wizard approached Nate.

Gripped with terror, Nate wanted to flee. He felt as if his feet were rooted to the floor. The Wizard reached him and dropped to one knee. Nate was flabbergasted.

With both hands, the Red Wizard raised the staff toward Nate. He bowed his head. "You have overcome that which is sin, mastering the art of self-discipline. Only the greatest would not fail. Time and time again you did prevail. Now take this Staff of Power within your hands. You'll be the greatest wizard throughout the lands."

Bewildered and still expecting to be punished for trespassing, Nate looked from the Wizard to the staff. His eyes returned to Wizard's sincere face.

"You've proven your greatness by conquering this tower. Only the greatest can control this staff's power."

I did conquer this tower! Nate was suddenly overcome with confidence. *I'll bet no one else ever has.* Feeling prouder than he had ever felt in his life, Nate puffed out his chest. He reached to take the staff. *If only my father was here to see this!* Nate glanced around the room.

All the walls around him were illuminating a soft violet glow. *Razzle!* Nate's arm froze in midair. The door he'd entered radiated the same violet.

"This is just another test, isn't it?" Nate lowered his arm. The wizard in front of him seemed to flicker. Nate squinted. He saw through the image. *It's not the real Wizard!*

Every vase in the room crashed to the floor, shattering upon impact. The petals of the delicate flowers whooshed together in a gentle whirlwind around Nate. Still kneeling before Nate, the

Wizard's mirage evaporated with a hiss into a column of steam and merged with the petals.

The rushing wind grew louder. The speed of the whirlwind increased. Trapped within the cyclone, Nate squeezed his eyes tightly shut and pulled his arms into his chest. He felt himself spinning around and around. He gagged, afraid he would vomit. The swirling stopped.

Stumbling to his knees, Nate caught himself with outstretched hands. He opened his eyes. When he could see clearly, he stood. He was just inside the door of a circular room different from all the others. *Could I really be at the top?*

"Red Wizard?" No one answered. Nate looked around.

The wall next to him held a painting of three young wizards. Each gripped a new wooden staff. Their only unique feature was their brown, blond, or red hair. An olive-skinned wizard with curly black hair stood proudly next to them. His staff looked worn from years of use.

Nate moved around the room. Shelves held corked jars of varying shapes and sizes filled with colorful potions. Some were liquid, others were

101

powder. Some were translucent while others were dense. Black clay floated within a bubbly, red liquid in a square jar. When Nate drew nearer, the black blob morphed into the silhouette of a tall, skinny boy. Nate chuckled.

The shelves of potions ended at an open window. A soft breeze ushered in the scent of the recent rainstorm. Nate took a refreshing breath. Bright sunshine spilled past sturdy darkoak shutters. A breathtaking view of the Greatfalls River stretched like a sparkling, silver ribbon from the peak of Gemstone Mountain to the glistening waters of Silver Lake. Nate had never seen this view of the countryside. He lingered for sometime before his curiosity pulled him away.

Bookshelves groaned with books of every size. Titles such as *The History of Wizardry*; *Dragons— A Wizard's Worst Nightmare*; and *Holy Spells Guaranteed to Ward Off Demons or Vanquish Vampires* intrigued Nate. He resisted the urge to pull a worn, leather-bound book entitled *Dontrud's Collection* from the shelf. He didn't need another hex. *I hope I didn't go through all this trouble for nothing. Where's the Red Wizard?* Nate wondered.

He continued to explore and discovered a crystal cabinet full of dozens of wands. He was surprised to see very few fancy wands. Most of them were wooden and looked very old. A purple raven landed on the sill of a window mirroring the one directly across the room. It stared at Nate as if questioning his presence. Nate stepped toward the window. The raven soared off into the panoramic view of Northern Versii.

The Crimson City contrasted boldly with the bordering waters of the Green Sea. The sea stretched from the coast until it disappeared at the horizon. Northwest of the Crimson City, sun rays reflected brilliantly off the Golden Mountains, where everything that grew seemed laced with gold.

Startled by movement from the corner of his eye, Nate spun around. A snowy-white cat bounded into a doorway. Nate had come nearly full circle. He approached the opened door of a simple yet elegant bedroom. The feline hissed, arching its back.

Backing away, Nate bumped into a burgundy chair next to an oversized redwood table. An embedded milky stone covered the table's surface. When Nate examined the stone, it seemed to melt and began to swirl. It settled into a clear, moving picture.

Nate gaped at Ted straddling a pegasus. He was flying over a body of silver water. A mischievous grin stole across Ted's face. He stood and bent his knees. He raised his hands above his head as if preparing to dive. The pegasus jerked, throwing him off its back. Ted fell like a rock, splatting into the lake with a belly flop. Nate roared with laughter.

"WHO DARES TO INVADE MY HOME?"

The entire room shook. Nate dove under the table. Books and potions flew off the shelves. The crystal cabinet flung open. Wands spewed across the room, ricocheting off the floor. Clouds of red smoke filled the air. Nate's eyes burned. He began to cough. As quickly as it started, the shaking stopped. The smoke dissipated and everything flew back to its proper shelf.

Pointing his staff under the table, the Red Wizard demanded, "Who are you and how did you get in here?"

"I-I-I'm Nathaniel McG-G-Gray," Nate stammered in horror. He climbed out from under the table and stood. "I c-c-came up the s-s-stairs."

The Wizard eyed Nate suspiciously. "I see you had fun in each of my rooms," he chortled. His voice was much friendlier. He lifted a deep purple potion from the shelf. Returning to Nate he said, "Pour this over your head."

"O-o-over my head?" Nate took the bottle.

"You heard me, I can't have you leaving here looking like such a mess."

Nate took a deep breath, pulled the bottle's stopper, and did as he was told. A deep purple powder encircled him. When the substance evaporated, Nate stared in awe. All evidence of his trials in the tower had disappeared from his body. His thumb and wrist looked normal. His clothes were clean and dry. His ankle felt better and a quick touch to his forehead told him the goose egg was gone. The magic potion even got rid of the stench!

"Holy Gold! That's amazing!"

"After all you've been through, it's the least I could do. What did you see in my seer stone that was so humorous?"

Nate remembered the swirly stone on the table. "It showed my brother being thrown from a pegasus."

"You must have been thinking of your brother, then. Why were you thinking of him when you were in here?" The Wizard swept his arm around the room.

"He's on the pegasus because he's trying to become a champion. He thinks I'm too scared to follow my dream."

"If you saw him fall, he's not on the pegasus anymore," the Wizard assured. "What is your desire?"

"I know you've taught wizards before and I-I-I want you to teach me." Nate stated bravely.

"A wizard? Are you a noble?"

"No, sir. But my grandfather was one of the first peasants to become a knight in our kingdom so I know things can change."

"That's true. Things can change, but I'm afraid to learn magic you must be able to read and write. Magic is difficult for even the most educated man to learn."

"But, I am educated. My mother taught me."

"Hmm," the Wizard rubbed his chin. "Your stuttering concerns me. Magic requires exactness. If you say something wrong—or too slow—it can be disastrous."

"Yeah, I learned that the hard way." Nate grinned, recalling his mishaps at the magic show. "I'm a hard worker. I'll do whatever it takes to stop stuttering."

"You definitely have an answer for everything," the Wizard replied, almost under his breath. His face hardened. "I'm afraid dark times are coming to Versii. I don't have time for an apprentice."

"I know about the war." Nate straightened his shoulders. "I want to be a wizard so I can help."

The Red Wizard appeared to think. He smiled. "There are a few older wizards I could consult.

Mind you, I'm not making any promises, but I'm intrigued by you. Now, the king is expecting me so you best be going."

The Wizard chanted and tapped his staff sharply on the floor. A whirlwind of colors encircled Nate. Suddenly he was sitting on the wet grass in front of the tower. A horse whinnied. Nate glanced toward the stables. His father was leaving.

"Father, wait up." Nate hollered, running to catch him.

His father stopped the wagon and looked down at Nate. "Ya're still here? Did ya take a nap while the storm passed?"

"I just talked to the Red Wizard!" Nate could barely contain his excitement.

"The Red Wizard ya say? And I suppose now he's goin' ta train ya ta be a wizard. Sounds like ya had quite a dream."

"More like a dream come true!" Nate jumped into the wagon.

Chapter Eleven

GRUMPY GOOBLER

"**M**other!" Nate stepped into the kitchen. "You'll never believe what I did."

"What's that, Nathanial?" Leaning over the fire, she stirred the cauldron.

"I went into the Wizard's tower and . . ."

"YER SOON TA BE CHAMPION SON HAS RETURNED!" Ted burst through the front door. He strutted into the kitchen.

Their father emerged from his bedroom. "What's all the ruckus?"

Their mother filled two bowls with stew from the cauldron. Handing the bowls to Nate, she pulled a purple reed out of Ted's tangled hair. "What's this?"

"Must've got that when I dove off the pegasus," Ted shrugged.

"More like flopped off," Nate muttered, placing the bowls on the table.

Their mother eyed Ted suspiciously.

Their father looked uncertain.

Grinning, Ted took two more filled bowls and set them on the table. "Ya should have seen me." He planted himself in his chair. Barely pausing to inhale bites of stew, he didn't spare any details of his adventure. Nate couldn't even get a word in to defend himself when Ted painted him as a coward. Nate glared at his brother.

His father chuckled. "It's about time ya used yer mischievous nature for something other than gettin' inta trouble."

His mother shook her head. "I shouldn't be surprised that you planned something like this. Thank goodness you weren't hurt." She yawned, "Oh my, it's late. We'd better get to bed."

"What about the tower?" Nate protested.

"We'll hear your story in the morning," his mother stated.

That night Nate dreamt he was back in the tower. He successfully avoided every temptation. When he met the Red Wizard, he stood tall without a smidge of proof that he'd been through the tower. At breakfast, he didn't even wait until they had all sat down.

"The rain was pouring down. I saw the lightning flash around the tower and realized Ted was right. I had to do something if I was ever going to become a wizard."

His family listened skeptically.

"Do not pass through the doors within, unless you possess self-discipline. You must overcome that which is sin or fail you will time and time again." Nate could barely stay in his seat.

"A poem?" Ted raised an eyebrow.

"Don't interrupt, Theodore," their mother scolded.

Nate continued. "The first room was empty until a table flew down from the ceiling." Describing this test, Nate could almost taste the chocolateberries. "In the next room, there was more gold than I could even imagine. It was great until the bits cracked opened and released huge spiders." Nate shivered at the memory.

"A flyin' table? Spiders crawlin' out of coins?" His father shifted in his seat. "That's a great story, Nathanial, but I've got ta get ta the castle. I'll have ta hear the rest later."

"I'm comin', too. Nordof and I are trainin' this morning."

"But I'm not done," Nate balked.

"I'd love to hear more, Nathanial." His mother stood as well, "but Mrs. Goobler's expecting you. You need to finish eating so you can get to your chores and studying."

Nate scowled. Slumping down in his chair, he finished his mulberry mush. After breakfast, he headed outside to milk their two-headed cow. Later, he stumbled through his studies. Around mid-morning, he moped out the front door, dawdling as much as possible along the way.

Burrowville was named for the numerous burrows dug into the base of the hill surrounding the White Castle. Nate passed many in good condition. *Razzle!* Mrs. Goobler's burrow contrasted sharply with the neighboring burrows.

Mrs. Goobler put Nate right to work. Over the next few days, he removed caked-on muck from the stones of the rounded dwelling, pulled weeds that had taken over the front walkway, and reseeded the shrubbery. He cleared away hundreds of spider webs, scraped layers of dirt off the kitchen floor, and scrubbed years of grime out of the old iron bathtub. Mrs. Goobler sat in her antique rocking chair reading her well-worn books.

Nate dreaded his next project. A cave-in had filled the spare bedroom several years earlier. After almost a week of hauling rocks and shoveling mud, every muscle in Nate's body ached.

"Is that room finally cleared?" Mrs. Goobler grumbled.

"Yes, ma'am." Nate forced a smile while hauling the last rock through the living room.

"Good. Mr. Rogenhammer will be here in the morning. Until then there's not much you can do so you're done for the day."

"Thank you, ma'am." Nate backed through the front door, grateful for his unexpected freedom.

Trudging across the dirt road, he heaved the last rock into a deep ravine. It crashed into the other stones. He rubbed his tired biceps then darted away.

"Blinkly!" Nate hollered to his friend who was practicing his angling in front of his house. Using elfish magic, the Gordenall's had transformed their dying yard into a garden paradise. Any one of their spells would have saved Nate a lot of time at Mrs. Goobler's home. Nate fought back a flair of jealousy.

"Nate?" Blinkly's line drooped when he paused mid-cast. "What are you doing here?"

"I got done early, let's go fishing!"

After a quick stop to get Nate's fishing gear, they started toward Silver Lake.

"I met the Red Wizard," Nate mentioned casually.

"When did this happen?" Blinkly demanded. "Tell me everything."

Finally! Someone believes me! Nate started at the very beginning. They wound along the trail. He described every magical detail, scary escape, and hilarious mishap.

Blinkly eyes were wide with admiration when they reached the lake. "So is he going to teach you?"

"He doesn't have time. But he said he'll try to find someone who does."

"That's great! I knew you could become a wizard."

"I don't know. Someone has to agree to teach a peasant and he says I've got to stop stuttering."

"He probably already has someone in mind." Blinkly said. "You'll stop stuttering when you gain confidence in yourself."

"Maybe you're right."

"Of course I'm right! Now let's catch a silver snapper!"

◆ ◆ ◆

Thibol Rogenhammer, or Scub as most of the townsfolk called him, was the inventor of scubry—a thick, black, quick-hardening paste. He was the halfling to call after a cave-in. In just three days, Nate and Scub smothered every nook and cranny of the exposed rock in Mrs. Goobler's spare bedroom with scubry. The room was ready for framing. That night, Nate washed black paste off his clothes and arms with a borrowed bar of Blinkly's dragon soap while Ted sharpened his sword.

"I'm tellin' ya, Nate," Ted said, "I'm right there at the top. I'm in the runnin' for the pegasus race for sure."

"Sounds like you're doing great," Nate sighed. "I wish I could be there."

"It'd be nice ta have someone cheerin' me on. Mother's only been ta a few events and Father hasn't made any yet."

"At least Scub thinks we'll be done soon. Mrs. Goobler said this is my last project." Nate set the soap aside and toweled off. "Maybe I'll make it to some of the tryouts after all."

"It's about time ya finished payin' for yer crimes," Ted chuckled. "That's what ya get for thinkin' ya can do magic like a wizard."

"Yep." Nate was too tired to be provoked. "I'm going to sleep."

Four days later, Nate stood with Scub in Mrs. Goobler's finished room. They were proud of their work. Even Mrs. Goobler, who insisted on a thorough inspection before paying Scub, wasn't able to find anything to gripe about. After Scub left, Nate waited in awkward silence.

"I hope you're not expecting to get paid, too," Mrs. Goobler snapped.

"No ma'am. I just wanted to make sure there was nothing else."

Mrs. Goobler slowly glanced around her living room. "I said you'd be finished when the room was complete. Your obligation is fulfilled. If you'd just hand me that book," she pointed at a wide book on the top shelf, "you are free to leave."

Nate reached for the book. It was heavy. It slipped from his hands. Hitting the ground, it fell open to a page showing two oversized jeweled coins. One coin bore five yellow gems as the petals of a golden flower. On the other, an emerald was crafted into a ferocious dragon's head. He quickly closed the book and handed it to Mrs. Goobler.

"Sorry about that."

He bolted for the door, hoping to never return.

Chapter Twelve

WAR ON THE HORIZON

Sitting cross-legged on his bed, Nate yawned. Orange moonlight beamed through partly opened shutters. He wanted to be sleeping. Ted sat at the foot of Nate's bed bragging about the crossbow competition that day. He'd shot a perfect score and another contender had completely missed his target twice.

"I'm definitely one of the top three now!" Ted boasted. "Tomorrow I'll be racin' through the sky on a pegasus."

"You'll need some sleep if you're going to do that," Nate interrupted.

"I suppose ya're right."

"I am. Good night." Nate stretched out his legs and pushed Ted off the bed.

Ted picked himself up off the floor and flicked Nate on the ear. "That's no way ta treat the next champion," he joshed, climbing into his own bed.

"It is if I'm the next wizard!" Nate slid under his blanket and closed his eyes.

Main Street was packed. Hundreds of competitors and their families were anxious to learn the outcome of the tryouts. Nate spotted Blinkly by the bakery and waved him over to join his family.

"It's nice of ya'll ta finally come show yer support," Ted chided over the crowd noise.

His father clicked his tongue. "Ya did just fine without us. Work around the kingdom doesn't stop for the tryouts."

"I wish it had!" Nate sighed.

Blinkly fell into step alongside him.

"Would ya look over there." Ted pointed across the street toward The Mungletuss Hotel. "That's the city boy I've been tellin' ya about. I think he's in first place." Nate, Blinkly, and Ted stepped to the side. "I should've known they'd stay at the fanciest hotel in town."

A confident, well-built elf with curly brown hair and an older, distinguished elf waited on the hotel steps. The stable hand brought them a shiny black pegasus with a red saddle.

"He's got his own pegasus!" Nate exclaimed.

"I'm not worried. I can still beat him," Ted shrugged. "We'd better get movin'."

Poor Ted, he doesn't stand a chance, Nate thought. He raised his eyebrows toward Blinkly.

Blinkly shook his head.

The three of them caught up with their family.

The crowd pushed toward the dirt field near the castle. Unlike the Banner Day festival, the field held only one tent. It stood next to a towering platform. Avoiding a roped-off area in front, thousands of Versiians sat on the grassy slope. The air buzzed with hundreds of conversations. Nate's family followed Ted through the crowd.

"There." Ted pointed up the incline.

Nordof waved them over.

"Nordof!" Ted plopped down next to him. "Ya ready ta see yer best friend become a champion?"

Nate's mother and father greeted Nordof's parents.

"Is Ted always this confident?" Blinkly asked Nate.

"Always."

Nate and Blinkly sat. An elf blew a war horn. Lord Brade stood at the top of the platform. The crowd listened.

"Welcome, my fellow Versiians." Lord Brade's deep voice carried over the field. "Rise for King Darwin!"

Everyone stood. King Darwin emerged from the tent. The crowd cheered. The ebony-skinned man wore golden mesh armor. A purple robe draped his powerful shoulders. A stately crown rested on his grey-speckled hair. King Darwin climbed the platform flanked by two champions and took his seat on a throne.

Lord Brade motioned for silence. "Now welcome our visitors from the kingdom of MaDrone. Queen Dyllian and her battle sage, General Triatun."

The centaur queen appeared at the tent's flap. The crowd cheered again. A silver robe flowed from her neck to her hooves. A ruby tiara hugged her dark-brown hair. She was followed by a black centaur plated from neck to hooves in silver armor. With the general at her side, the queen positioned herself next to King Darwin.

Lord Brade once again gestured for the crowd to be silent. "Over the last eight days, our competitors have endured grueling tests of strength, dexterity, and endurance. They have displayed proficiency using all manner of weaponry and demonstrated intelligence in every area of warfare. Today these competitors will learn of their placement in the King's Royal Army.

"Because the King's Army is a volunteer army, you need to know that war is coming to our land." Lord Brade surveyed the crowd. "Even as we speak, the Red Wizard and a band of champions are assisting the inhabitants of MaDrone. They have fallen prey to a great evil and seek refuge. They are welcome in Versii."

The crowd murmured.

Nate shot Blinkly an uneasy look. His friend nodded.

"The army that viciously attacked MaDrone will eventually attack Versii. I've asked General Triatun to address you. General Triatun."

The crowd remained silent. The centaur stepped to the front of the podium. In a strong voice, General Triatun began, "Thank you Lord Brade. Over the past year, Versii has provided food, weapons, and gold to MaDrone with the hope that we would defeat our enemy. Once it became clear that this was not possible, the Red Wizard and several champions began helping our people escape. On behalf of Queen Dyllian and all of MaDrone, we thank King Darwin for his incredible generosity."

General Triatun nodded to the king.

King Darwin returned the nod with a solemn look.

General Triatun continued, "The best way for you to understand this evil is to show you a recent battle. Vamera—Vamata—Alamra!" The general waved his battle staff high above his head. It was a unique weapon, half wooden staff and half golden spear.

A crystal-clear picture appeared in a cloud above the podium. A lanky elf drove a black chariot pulled by four black lions with blood-red manes. Nate shivered at the sight of King Siddon.

King Siddon cracked a fiery whip. The crowd jumped. The image panned out. Siddon's massive army was revealed—elves riding lions with blood-red manes; imps of various sizes, shapes, and species; and burgundy lava dragons hovering overhead. The crowd gasped.

When the picture panned out further the army's target was revealed. A stunning ruby-red castle stood in the distance. The picture zoomed in and focused on thousands of armed centaurs and satyrs behind the castle walls. They waited to defend themselves against Siddon's approaching army.

The picture widened. Siddon's army charged the castle. The defenders launched arrows and spears into the air. Burning rocks and destroyers—spiked iron balls—were launched from catapults. Hot oil poured over the castle walls, scalding the invaders.

"Ala—Maham!" General Triatun waved his spear through the image. The battle scene disappeared. The cloud evaporated.

"The outcome of that battle was devastating. Our castle was destroyed. Most of our brave warriors were killed. The actions of your king averted a greater tragedy. Our civilians had been evacuated before the battle. They are en route to Versii. Our people and what is left of our army are eternally indebted to you. We pledge to help defend your great kingdom."

The crowd remained silent. Everyone seemed to be trying to make sense of what they had just learned. General Triatun returned to stand next to Queen Dyllian.

Lord Brade stepped forward. "King Darwin is working with General Triatun and other leaders to develop a defense strategy against this army. You have seen what is coming to our land. You must decide—are you willing to join in defending your kingdom?"

The crowd shouted "Yes!"

Lord Brade's face looked grave. "We have made tryout changes that will strengthen our army. The pegasus race has been eliminated."

An uneasy hush fell over the crowd. Ted's mouth gaped.

Lord Brade continued, "Although the pegasus race has been eliminated, the top three competitors have been identified. When I call your names, join me on the platform."

Nate glanced quickly at Ted whose gaze was fixated on Lord Brade.

"The top overall performer is Jondor Kerillian from the Crimson City." The "city boy" strutted toward the podium. The crowd cheered. Lord Brade continued, "Next, Eria Whiteheart from the Shifty Desert." The crowd cheered for an athletic young lady making her way to the podium.

Nate and Ted held their breath.

"The third and final top performer," Lord Brade announced, "is our very own Theodore McGray from Burrowville."

The crowd roared. Ted jumped to his feet. Through a wave of enthusiastic pats on his back, he rushed toward the platform. Joining the other two competitors next to Lord Brade, the three exchanged looks of wonderment.

Lord Brade motioned for the crowd to settle down. "Because we need as many warriors as possible to fight in the impending war, King Darwin will appoint all three of these competitors as champions—if they will accept the assignment."

Ted, Jondor, and Eria stared at each other. They turned enthusiastically to Lord Brade, proclaiming, "We accept!"

"Very well." Lord Brade faced the king. "King Darwin, I present these three fine warriors to you."

King Darwin rose. The three knelt before him. The crowd was reverent. Assisted by his squire, one by one, King Darwin placed a black helmet with decorative golden wings on the heads of each of the three competitors. He instructed them to stand.

"Each of you has been selected to serve as a champion for the kingdom of Versii," King Darwin declared. "Do you swear to always fight valiantly, nobly, and loyally for your kingdom?"

"We do!" the three answered.

"I proclaim you to be the newest champions of Versii!"

The crowd shouted their approval. King Darwin motioned for the new champions to take their places behind his throne. Captain Goobler and several other captains joined Lord Brade on the platform. The crowd quieted.

Lord Brade stated, "If your name is read by one of the captains, come to the roped-off area."

Captain Goobler replaced Lord Brade at the podium. He read a list of names from a parchment. The other captains followed suit. To Nate's surprise, when the captains were finished, numerous competitors, including Derik and his gang, had not been selected.

The crowd began to mumble. Lord Brade continued. "To maximize the strength of our army, we are reinstating the foot soldier. This soldier will wield the polearm." He raised a wooden pole with a three-pronged head: spiked hammer, spear, and axe. "Training in hand-to-hand combat will prepare the foot soldier for battle on the front lines. We invite all remaining competitors to join us as foot soldiers."

The eerily silent crowd waited. A single voice bellowed, "I'll do it!"

Nate turned toward the voice. He couldn't believe his eyes. The crowd roared.

Derik—the biggest coward Nate knew— approached the platform. Derik's thugs followed him, declaring they, too, would become foot soldiers. The crowd roared even louder. Soon all the remaining competitors joined Derik.

Lord Brade silenced the crowd. "The time will come when we all will fight fiercely to defend our kingdom. But tonight we celebrate our allegiance to Versii!"

Nate's head spun. Ted was a champion, Derik was a town hero, and Versii was preparing for war.

Chapter Thirteen

AN UNEXPECTED VISITOR

Nate sucked down his lunch of mollypog soup. Why would anyone think these slimy worms are a delicacy?

"Finish up." His mother interrupted his thoughts. "You need to go to the Bird Man's house to help your sister with her bags."

"Yes, ma'am." Nate jumped up.

After a morning of cleaning, Nate was ready to get out of the house. Their mother was driving herself and everyone else crazy preparing for Ted's going-away party that night. His sister's visit, paid for from Ted's salary advance, added to their mother's excitement and anxiety.

Jogging across town, he paused at Main Street to allow several cavalry riders and an armored war wagon to pass. To his surprise, the wagon stopped right in front of him. The door swung open. Thorton Brade stepped out.

The last time Nate had seen Thorton, he was a huge blob in the infirmary. He couldn't be more different now. His body was back to its normal slightly plump shape, his long red hair was slicked back, and he wore a fancy tunic. He carried a golden staff and strutted up to Nate with more confidence than Nate would expect from a king.

"Nathanial," Thorton jutted out his chin. "You'll be interested to know, I have been selected by King Darwin himself to train as our kingdom's next wizard at the Halls of Magic."

"So that's why you were mad at me." Thorton had been Nate's friend until he found out Nate wanted to be a wizard.

"Not that it matters," Thorton mocked. "A peasant like you never stood a chance."

"Maybe you're right." Nate pressed his lips together.

"Of course I'm right!" Thorton whipped around. Climbing inside the wagon, he shut the door. "Let's go!" The driver snapped the reins. Nate was left in their dust.

Life just isn't fair. I would be a better wizard than Thorton! Flustered, Nate broke into a sprint. He didn't stop until he reached the Bird Man's house.

The Bird Man, an elf properly known as Pidan Longbrow, could get anyone anywhere in the kingdom on his rainbow soarer. It easily carried three grown men. Slowing to a brisk walk, Nate followed a stone pathway that led around Longbrow's two-story home. He entered a lush backyard lined with plum trees.

Nate approached a motherly elf picking plums. "Excuse me. I'm looking for the Bird Man."

"I'm expecting him soon. You can wait over there." She pointed toward a barn behind the trees.

"Thanks." Nate continued along the path. He was about to sit down in a hickory chair next to the barn when he heard high-pitched shrieking overhead.

With its enormous wings fully spread, the rainbow soarer floated out of the sky. It landed gracefully and took a few steps toward the barn. When the soarer lay on her belly, the Bird Man slid out of the saddle's front seat. He retrieved a step stool next to the barn and placed it under the second seat for Nate's sister, Denya.

Denya sat side-saddle on the soarer. She slid down, stepping with confidence and dignity onto the stool. Her strawberry-blonde hair was twisted up in a bun and secured with several long sticks. Her sparkling green dress touched her knees. The laces on her green sandals wrapped up her shins. Nate met her at the stool. He helped her off with a bear hug.

"Look at you, Nate. You must have grown two boot-lengths in the last year," Denya said.

"What about you? You don't look like you're from Burrowville anymore!"

"Thanks!" Denya brushed her dress with her hands. "Will you get my bags?" She pointed at several leather bags strapped into the third seat. While the Bird Man cared for the soarer, Nate moved the stool and retrieved the bags.

"Did you bring enough stuff?" Nate teased, hoisting a large bag over each shoulder and a hand bag around his neck. He lifted the two remaining small bags in each hand.

"You don't have to carry them all, silly." Denya lifted the hand bag from around his neck. She took the smaller of the two bags from his hands and called, "Thank you, Mr. Longbrow, it was a wonderful flight."

"You're welcome." The Bird Man brushed the soarer's wings. "See you next week."

"It's great to have you home, Denya." Nate followed her through the plum trees. Denya always encouraged Nate to share his dreams with her. He was happy to have some time alone with her. "I have so much to tell you."

"And I have so much to tell you," Denya replied. "The last year has been full of adventures!"

Denya talked nonstop about her experiences in the Redwood Forest. She was being taught to be an accomplished handmaiden and a proper lady.

Nate tried to hide his frustration while she droned on. They crossed the bridge at the entrance of the Darkoak Forest. Denya finished her story about how she had heroically saved a white troll—apparently the only friendly type— who had barely escaped after being attacked by lumberwolves.

"Looks like it was good you were there for him." *And thank you for finally telling an interesting story*, Nate thought.

"So what did you want to tell me?" she asked.

They rounded the corner near home. Their wagon was parked in front of the house. "It looks like Father's home early. I'll have to tell you later," Nate sighed.

"Just don't forget. I want to hear everything," Denya said over her shoulder. She darted as fast as her fitted skirt allowed toward the house. Nate reached the top step with the heavy bags. Denya's voice carried from inside the house. "Why are you crying, mother?"

Mother never cries. Nate scrunched his eyebrows. Entering the front hall, he set the bags down. A wide-eyed Denya stood next to their parents seated on the bench.

"What's wrong?" Nate asked uneasily.

"Ya have a visitor." His father's voice was husky. He nodded toward the rocking chair.

Shutting the door, Nate turned around slowly. Rocking comfortably in their modest home was the Red Wizard. Nate jumped back in astonishment, tumbling over the bags.

"H-h-hello, sir." Nate picked himself up off the floor.

"Hello, Nathanial." The Red Wizard smiled. "Why don't we go for a walk?" Leaning on his wooden staff, the Red Wizard rose from the rocker. He took a step toward Nate's family. "Thank you for welcoming me into your home."

"It was an honor." Nate's father sat up even taller.

"Mrs. McGray, you have raised wonderful children. I am confident they will continue to excel. Thank you for the sacrifices your family is making for our kingdom."

Nate's mother wiped a fresh tear from her eye. "It's not easy to see them grow up, but I'm proud of who they're becoming."

"You have reason to be. Speaking of children, you must be Denya. I see the Redwood Elves are treating you well."

"Yes . . . sir." Denya struggled to answer.

The Red Wizard turned to Nate, gesturing to the door. "Shall we?"

Nate held the door open. His thoughts raced.

The Red Wizard led Nate between the billow bird coop and the garden. "I've always loved the Darkoak Forest. You are fortunate to live so close."

Nate made an effort to not stutter. "Yes, sir."

They came to a small opening within the forest. The Wizard sat on a dead tree. He motioned for Nate to join him.

"I found a wizard willing to teach you."

Nate was stunned.

The Wizard grinned. "Tomorrow you will travel to the Crimson City to join Thorton Brade. The King's Army will escort you to the Halls of Magic."

"But why?" Nate didn't know what else to say.

"Over the years, many of the nobles selected by King Darwin have failed to complete their wizard training. We need someone who can assist me in serving the kingdom. You are the only individual to ever conquer the challenges in my tower. You have proven you have the determination and integrity to be a great wizard.

"When I told my mentor, Master Loperian, about you, he agreed you deserve a chance. He will take you on as one of his apprentices."

Nate was speechless.

"These are uncertain times. I would've preferred to have your party flown to the Halls of Magic but Thorton refuses to fly." Nate thought he saw the Wizard's lips tighten ever so slightly. "As an extra precaution, your journey tomorrow morning begins with a visit to the alchemist."

Nate found his voice. "But, isn't the alchemist crazy?"

"Perhaps," the Red Wizard chuckled. "He is also a good friend of mine. His potions will protect you on your journey. Lady Gordenall will see you to the alchemist and then to the Crimson City."

"Lady Gordenall?"

"Yes, your friend, Danzandorian, will join you at the Halls to study elfish magic."

Nate beamed. This was even better than he could've imagined.

"I will send word for Thorton to wait for you at the King's Dock. His escort party will see the three of you safely to the Halls. Any questions?"

Nate was sure he had questions but his mind was spinning so fast he simply answered, "No, sir."

"Very well." The Red Wizard stood and reached into his cloak. "I'm entrusting you with a special gift." He handed Nate a weathered wooden wand.

Suddenly, images of Mrs. Goobler falling off the stage bombarded Nate's mind. He tried to hide his uncertainty. "What does it do?"

"Point it at that stump and yell Snare—Eran."

Nate took aim. "Snare—Ran." Nothing happened.

"Snare—*Eran*," the Red Wizard gently reminded him.

"Snare—E-e-eran." A blue substance sputtered from the wand, falling at Nate's feet.

"Relax and concentrate before you speak. Try it one more time."

Nate inhaled. *Snare—Eran. Snare—Eran. Snare—Eran.* He exhaled slowly. "Snare-Eran!"

Thick, dark-blue goo shot from the wand. It clung to the base of the stump and enveloped it, hardening immediately.

The Red Wizard nodded his approval. "That stump is now trapped until freed by the strongest magic. You're only to use the wand if your life is in danger. Keep it somewhere safe, but have it ready when needed."

"Of course, sir!" Nate was in awe. He glanced down at the wand. "Sir," he hesitated, "I just thought of a question."

"What is it?"

"This wand. I didn't expect it to be so powerful. There were so many amazing-looking wands in the green room in your tower. Why is this one so . . . plain?"

"Wands, like people," the Wizard gently explained, "cannot be judged by their outward appearances. Most fancy wands are good for tricks but not for saving a life."

"I see. Thank you."

"Unless you have any other questions, it's time for me to go."

"No, sir."

"In that case, may fortune smile upon you during your journey. Al—May—Bestafy." The Wizard was gone.

Nate eyed the blue stump. He had successfully performed his first spell! He stared again at the wand—*his* wand. Tucking it safely within the side of his boot, he started toward home.

Chapter Fourteen

THE ALCHEMIST

"The Wizard tapped his staff on the floor." Nate had his family's undivided attention. "Suddenly there were bright colors all around me and I magically appeared on the grass outside the tower. That is when I saw . . ." A rapping sound on the front door interrupted Nate. Sunlight peeked through the slits in the shutters. "Is it morning already?"

Nate and his family moved to the front hall. When Nate opened the door, Blinkly stepped inside with his mother, Lady Gordenall.

"Did you sleep at all last night?" Blinkly eyed Nate.

"No." Nate grinned at his family. "They could barely wait until the party was over to hear about the Wizard's tower."

Nate's mother's eyes were misty. She took Lady Gordenall's hand in her own. "Thank you for seeing our sons to the Crimson City. I couldn't send Nathanial off completely alone."

"It's my pleasure." Lady Gordenall touched her shoulder. "It's also a bit selfish. I couldn't handle it myself."

The McGray's followed the Gordenall's outside. Nate hugged his mother and Denya and got three hugs in return. Breaking away, he squeezed his misty-eyed father and turned to Ted.

"You be careful out there, Ted." Nate sounded playful to hide his raw emotions. "Those pegasi can knock your teeth out."

"Ya'd better stay out of trouble, too, little brother." Ted suddenly grabbed Nate in a massive bear hug. "I won't be there ta save yer hide."

Nate, Blinkly, and Lady Gordenall settled into an elegant carriage assembled from colorful pine branches. The elf coachman snapped the reins of six red-antlered stags. Waving goodbye, Nate choked back tears.

The carriage rolled through Burrowville. They reached a highly traveled dirt road that snaked throughout the kingdom. A wooden sign read:

Nate groaned inside. It should've read "Maduman Highway," but the sign was a source of constant pranks. Each time it was repaired, the same letters were removed, showing how many of the citizens of Burrowville felt about the alchemist who lived atop a nearby path. The carriage came to a stop at the bottom of the hill.

"Why so fidgety?" Blinkly asked Nate.

"The alchemist is crazy."

"My father's favorite blacksmith was insane but he still made the finest weapons." Blinkly grinned.

"Don't dawdle, boys," Lady Gordenall instructed. "The escort party is expecting us to arrive before dusk."

With the crisp autumn breeze ruffling their hair, Nate and Blinkly reached the top of the hill. A circular, three-story building constructed of iron and cement loomed in front of them. Smoke puffed from a metal chimney. An oversized, copper cylinder protruded from the roof.

"Anyone living in there must be mad," Blinkly jested.

Nate rolled his eyes. Snarling sounded near the home. Nate tensed. The snarling changed to a whimper. A three-headed creature limped toward them.

"Demon!" Nate and Blinkly ran to the animal, scratching behind his ears as Demon eagerly licked their faces.

Blinkly rubbed Demon's splinted leg. "What happened?"

"He was caught in a trap." A round-faced man, whose hair had receded to tufts of white behind his ears, emerged from the house. "I'm Birchtran, the Alchemist. You must be Nathanial and Danzandorian." Birchtran eyed the boys through crude spectacles fashioned out of iron and two oversized crystals that made his eyes appear three times larger than normal.

"Yes, sir." Nate turned from Demon. "Thank you for helping our friend. Did you see the Trapper?"

"He showed up just as I was releasing the trap. I couldn't stand his ranting. I used a potion to transform him into a silver stag. For one week, he got to see what it's like to be hunted." Birchtran pressed his spectacles up the bridge of his chubby nose. "We'd better hurry. Time's a wasting."

"I like him already." Blinkly patted Demon's wolf head one more time.

"So do I." Nate followed Blinkly inside. Birchtran led the boys through a cluttered foyer into a circular, two-story workshop.

Nate and Blinkly stared at a gigantic iron contraption. Copper pipes and spiraling glass tubing protruded from its top and sides. Birchtran threw open two hefty boiler doors at its base. The room filled with sweltering heat. Nate wiped his brow. Birchtran shoveled coal into the flames and secured the door shut. The room cooled as quickly as it had heated up.

"Squaaaaaaaawk!" A bright green bird with bat-like wings flew down from the ceiling and perched on top of Birchtran's head. Nate and Blinkly jumped. Birchtran didn't even flinch.

Does he even know the bird is there? Nate raised his eyebrow to Blinkly.

They followed Birchtran to a wooden table covered with bowls, cylinders, flasks, canisters, and cauldrons.

"Where's the red bowl? Where is it?" Birchtran muttered while sorting through stacks of metal bowls. "Where . . . ah, here it is." Clearing a space with his arm, Birchtran placed the deepest bowl flat on the table. From a tin flask, he poured in a silver liquid. He mumbled, "What did I do with the aquatary leafs, I just had them here, right here. Where did they go? Oh . . . that's right I sat them over here." He grabbed a wooden bucket, counted out seven small purple leaves, and dropped them into the bowl.

Something brushed against Nate's leg. He flinched. It was a creature that could've been a cat if it had fur or whiskers.

"Now I need your hair," Birchtran suddenly commanded amidst his rambling. He faced Nate and Blinkly.

"Why?" Nate feared he would soon be as hairless as the poor cat.

"Invisibility potions are tailored to the recipient."

"Recipient?" Nate looked at Blinkly.

"To you." Birchtran plucked several strands of Nate's hair.

"Ouch!" Nate jumped back, scaring the bald cat away.

Blinkly grinned. He seemed to enjoy the chaos. He pulled some of his own hair out and handed it to Birchtran.

"That should do. Now the unicorn droppings," Birchtran tossed the boys' hairs into the bowl and began searching though the containers.

"Droppings?" Blinkly's smile faded.

"Yes, droppings. How else would you harvest the magical properties hidden inside a unicorn?" Birchtran rummaged through the jars on the table. "Where did it go?" He felt under the table. His expression softened. "Oh, here it is."

Birchtran uncorked a round jug. The pungent odor of dung made Nate inhale sharply. He held his breath. Birchtran scooped a ladle full of unicorn manure into the bowl and replaced the jug's cork. Nate exhaled.

"Open the refiner." Birchtran nodded at a handle beside Nate.

Nate opened the door. It screeched. Nate cringed. The batty bird flew off Birchtran's head. Birchtran dumped the bowl's contents into the refiner. Cradling the empty bowl in his arm, he pressed the door closed.

With a grinding noise, the machine began shaking. A thin paste shot up, over, around, and down through the glass tubing. Birchtran picked

151

up an empty jar with a fat round bottom and a thin neck. When the refiner stopped shaking, he placed the jar under a nozzle, pulled a lever, and filled the jar with the bubbling liquid.

"This invisibility potion is designed for the two of you alone." Birchtran corked the bottle and handed it to Nate. "Drinking half of it will make you invisible for one full day."

"Drinking it?" Nate gulped. The stench of manure still filled his nostrils.

"Yes, drinking it." Birchtran seemed puzzled by the question.

Shrugging his shoulders at Blinkly, Nate tucked the potion in his knapsack between his extra shirt and his wool pants.

"The potions you are receiving are very valuable. I'd normally charge four gold bits for all of them, but I'll give them to you for half that since you were sent here by my best customer. Now where did I put the other two?" Birchtran rubbed his chin. "That's right, I put them in the back room." He led Nate and Blinkly into another room.

Parchments littered a table, a few chairs, and the surrounding floor. Two potions sat on top of the mess. Nate recognized the first—the red liquid from the Wizard's tower. Birchtran reached for the flask. The floating, black clay transformed and looked like Birchtran's round head. He handed it to Blinkly. The lump became a stocky elf.

"When this bottle is emptied, the potion will create an illusion of whatever you're imagining," Birchtran explained. "Be warned, if your attackers aren't scared off, they can walk right through it. Make it count!"

"Got it!" Nate and Blinkly replied in unison.

"This is the best healing potion there is." Birchtran handed Blinkly a miniature jar filled with a bright-pink liquid.

Blinkly placed both potions in his leather pack and paid for them.

"My own blend of lava spices makes it's hot. That's why your friend Demon won't swallow it. Three drops will fix any wound unless it's from a cursed weapon or if you're dead." Birchtran polished his spectacles with his shirt. "So don't die—got it?"

"Yes sir!" Nate said. *He may be a little crazy but I can't argue with his advice.*

Chapter Fifteen

THE CRIMSON CITY

The Gordenall's carriage approached the final slope of their journey. The picturesque skyline unfolded along the coast of the sparkling Green Sea. The Crimson City was one of the busiest ports in Zndaria. Buildings towered above a heavily fortified, crimson clay wall. Their party joined the masses passing through the city's gates. The wall masked their surroundings.

The din of clomping horse hooves, squeaking wheels, and non-stop chatter was only slightly muffled within the carriage. A gang of gypsies sparkled in their brightly adorned outfits. A band of nomads exited the city riding on the backs of five-humped camels. Just inside the gates, their carriage driver waited while a group of heavily armed dwarfs herded mules burdened with bulky leather packs.

Winding their way through the city, Nate was fascinated. Wagons, carts, chariots, coaches, and carriages were pulled by every sort of creature from horses to giant rodents. Individuals dressed in colorful clothing hustled in and out of buildings. They barely acknowledged each other in passing. Entertainers on street corners played bizarre musical instruments, performed dangerous stunts, or attempted basic magic tricks.

"Whoa!" Nate chuckled, pointing to a halfling sporting a bright orange tunic, a spiky purple mohawk, and silver chain earrings that touched the halfing's shoulders.

"Have you been to the city before?" Lady Gordenall asked.

"I've never left Burrowville!"

"Wait until we get to the port market," Blinkly said. "It's like you're in a completely different world."

Blinkly was right. Passing through the port market, Nate spied a brown-skinned cyclops bartering for a nose ring; a shirtless, tattooed elf swapping black-sea fish for wool; and a group of slanted-eye centaurs buying bottles of purple minerals. A band of albino dwarfs sold glistening gems, and three burly women purchased spears. A stout treeman attempted to trade a dazzling pearl necklace for a feisty panther.

At the docks, a group of muscular black satyrs with dreadlocks heaved barrels off a cargo vessel. Boarians, hairy creatures with human bodies and boar heads, repaired a longship. A high, bronze wire fence near the end of the port enclosed the King's Dock. A dozen of his majesty's warships floated regally in the bay.

"Thank you, Lady Gordenall." Nate opened the carriage door. Salty sea air filled his nostrils. Hundreds of small, grey birds flying overhead screeched high-pitched greetings.

"You're welcome. I'll be at the Marryweather Inn if you need me for any reason." Lady Gordenall squeezed Blinkly one last time. "Write me as soon as you arrive at the Halls safely."

"I will. I promise. Love you!" Blinkly pecked his mother on the check and snatched his pack. The boys stepped out of the carriage.

At the gate, Nate showed the guard a royal parchment.

"The end of the third dock." The guard pointed to his right.

"Thank you," Nate said. They started toward the dock. "Have you been to the Halls before?"

"Once when I was little," Blinkly explained. "I played in the garden with my father while my mother studied."

A knight on the third dock approached them. "May I help you?"

"I'm Nathanial McGray. This is Danzandorian Gordenall. We're here by order of the Red Wizard

158

to join Thorton Brade's party." Nate handed him the parchment.

The knight examined the parchment. He looked confused. "Lord Brade's son and his guards sailed out this morning."

"What? B-b-but the Red Wizard sent word he was to wait for us."

"A champion did arrive with a message. Young Lord Brade said it instructed him to leave immediately."

"No!" Nate stomped the ground in anger. "That's a rotten trick, even for Thorton. Now what are we going to do?"

"When does the next ship travel to Taycod?" Blinkly asked.

"Not for few weeks, unless I receive an order from the king."

"Doesn't that count?" Nate pointed to the parchment.

"This states you will join the Brade escort party," the knight handed the parchment back to Nate, "not that we'll provide you your own."

Nate's mouth gaped. His face burned. He jammed the parchment back into his pack.

"Come on, Nate." Blinkly tugged on Nate's arm. "Let's go see if my mother can help."

Nate furrowed his eyebrows. The sun drooped. He followed Blinkly past the guarded gate. If Nate's memory was correct, the tropical-themed Marryweather Inn was located at the entrance of the port market.

Transporting himself by blinking, Blinkly moved ahead then waited for Nate to catch up. Running past the dwindling vendors of the port market, Nate stumbled over something in his path. He caught himself with his outstretched hands on the hard ground. Someone tugged on his back. He flipped over. A masked figure shrouded in black darted away with his knapsack.

"Stop!" Nate jumped to his feet, wiping his bloody, scraped hands on his pants.

Blinkly appeared suddenly. "What happened?"

"He stole my bag!" Nate hollered, pointing at the figure running around a pile of planks into a dark alley. "We have to get it back. It has my extra clothes and the invisibility potion." Nate started running.

"Don't worry, we'll catch him." Blinkly disappeared, reappearing at the entrance of the alley. When Nate reached him, Blinkly pointed into the darkness. "He went between those buildings. Let's go!"

Blinkly disappeared, leaving Nate to feel his way down the alley. Nate was furious someone had stolen his pack. His eyes adjusted to the dark. Blinkly waited up ahead. Nate joined him.

"He's looking through your stuff," Blinkly whispered, pointing around the building. "On three, I'll get him—you get the bag."

"Got it." Nate was ready.

"One, two." Blinkly disappeared.

Nate darted around the corner.

The black figure spun around and kicked Blinkly squarely in the chest. Blinkly flew several boot-lengths, bowling over a cluster of tin trash cans with a clatter.

Nate charged from behind. The thief twisted high into the air, kicking Nate in the side of the head. Grabbing his throbbing ear, Nate fell to his knees. The bandit flung the pack over his shoulder. He flipped over a pile of debris and dashed around another corner.

Blinkly pulled himself from under the pile of trash cans. "No one does that to me!" He blinked himself to the corner. "C'mon, let's get him."

Nate scrambled to his feet. His anger faded. He realized they could be in danger. Pulling his wand from his boot, he followed Blinkly around the corner. The thief was gone.

"Where'd he go?"

"I don't know." Blinkly's jaw was tight, his fists clenched. "He just disappeared!"

"Maybe he used the potion."

"It wouldn't work for him, remember?" Blinkly's fists relaxed. "At least I still have the healing and imagery potion."

Nate spotted bright lights at the end of the alley. "We'd better get out of the dark."

Nate kept his wand ready until they reached the busy street. They were no longer in the port market. Filigree lamps lined the street. Each lamp held a star-shaped candle burning at all five points.

"Let's find the Marryweather Inn before we have any more problems," Nate said.

Strolling along the crowded cobblestone sidewalk, Nate and Blinkly asked for directions. Individuals dressed in fine clothing looked at them with distain. Others, dressed in clothes so ragged even Nate's mother wouldn't let him wear, acted indifferent. No one would bother with them.

Blinkly stopped. He pointed across the street to a sign that read:

> ## MILLIGANS
> ### THE FINEST TUNICS, JERKINS, AND HOUPPELANDES A NOBLEMAN CAN BUY!

"Let's ask them for directions. They'll be glad to help after we buy you some new clothes," Blinkly said.

"What's wrong with these?" Nate looked down. A skinned knee peeked through a hole in his patched, blood-smeared pants.

Blinkly chuckled, "You don't have a change of clothes. Besides if you're going to be a wizard, you need to look like one."

A halfling maneuvered six black bears pulling an extended carriage with twelve curtained windows down the street. After it passed, Nate and Blinkly rushed over to the candle-lit window. Several wooden figures were dressed in fine clothing.

"I don't think I belong in there," Nate protested.

"Sure you do. You're a wizard. Remember that makes you better than a nobleman." Blinkly pushed him toward the shop.

"I'm not a wizard yet."

"They don't know that."

Slouching, Nate followed Blinkly through the shiny gold-plated doors. A tall, sharply dressed elf approached them.

"Are you boys in the right place?" The elf looked down his nose at them.

Nate glanced at Blinkly, sure the elf would kick them out.

Blinkly slipped the elf a silver bit. "I need to purchase some clothing for my friend here."

"Yes, you do." The elf eyed Nate's clothing and shuddered. He seemed to force a smile. "We can make anyone look modish." Sliding the bit into his pocket, the elf clapped twice.

Two halflings emerged from the back and ushered Nate to a changing room. They bustled away, returning with an assortment of clothing Nate felt was far too fancy. He finally settled on two pairs of wool pants (discovered in the basement), several long-sleeved cotton shirts, and a tan jerkin.

Wearing one set of new clothing, Nate stood tall in front of the mirror. He was used to second-hand clothes. These clothes seemed to shine. He grinned. He placed the extra items in a new leather backpack. Blinkly paid the shopkeeper and handed Nate a leather pouch.

Nate peered inside the pouch. It was full of gold, silver and bronze bits. "I can't take this. I can't even pay you back for these clothes."

"You don't have to. I'm helping pay your way to the Halls. You need to have money in case we get separated." Blinkly walked out the door before Nate could protest.

Nate peeked inside the pouch once more before securing it in a pocket inside his jerkin. He followed Blinkly outside into the crowd. His clothes made him feel confident. The pouch of coins made him more cautious. He held his new pack tightly and stayed next to Blinkly.

"The inn should be over just a few streets." Blinkly steered them across the road.

"'Ey, boys, over 'ere."

Nate and Blinkly looked into the shadows between the two buildings they were passing. A thin man was draped in a dark cloak that revealed only his bulging, blood-shot eyes and long shallow face.

"C'n I interest yous in a fairy stick?"

"No!" Blinkly's sharpness surprised Nate. "Those things mess with your head." Blinkly pulled Nate away. They sped up, cutting through to the next street.

Nate stopped. He pointed at a sign over a green door. "It's the Green Door Tavern."

"Soooo?" Blinkly questioned.

"That's Helmore's family's tavern. They moved here about a year ago. Let's go in." Nate pushed through the door.

Bright candles in oval orbs dangling from the rafters cast a green glow throughout the noisy tavern. A satyr playing a flute danced a silly jig. The tavern patrons talked and laughed. At the bar along the back wall, a bulky, bald fellow filled mugs of bubbler.

Helmore came out of the backroom carrying a tray of food. He was tall and thin like Nate, but his elf ears stuck out of his curly hair. He added several drinks to his tray and headed to a table of four women with human bodies and colorful wings.

"Follow me." Nate worked his way through the maze of tables.

Helmore placed the last platter—bearing a steaming octopus tentacle cut down the middle with a serving of fried sweet onions—in front of one of the ladies.

"Helmore!" Nate called.

Helmore spun around, his eyes and nose scrunched together.

"Nate?" Helmore exclaimed in surprise. "What are ya doin' here?"

"It's a long story." Nate noticed the ladies watching them.

"Let's go over ta the bar." Helmore guided them away. "I'll get ya something ta drink while ya tell me about it." He chuckled, "I almost didn't recognize ya. I've never seen ya lookin' so fancy."

"Thanks," Nate grinned. They reached the bar. Nate motioned to Blinkly. "Helmore, I'd like you to meet Blinkly. He moved to Burrowville a month ago."

"Nice ta meet ya, Blinkly. What brings ya two ta the Crimson City?" Helmore filled two glasses with mulberry juice.

"We're supposed to be on our way to Taycod but Thorton Brade left us stranded at the King's Dock." Blinkly took his glass from Helmore.

"That sounds like Thorton, still a little weasel." Helmore leaned against the counter facing them. "Taycod's a long way from Burrowville. What's in Taycod?"

"The Halls of Magic." Nate watched Helmore carefully. "I'm on my way to study to become a wizard."

"Holy Gold!" Helmore jumped back. "I knew you didn't want to be a woodsman but a *wizard*? How'd you manage that?"

"That's an even longer story, but we can't stay to tell it. We need to get to the Marryweather Inn. Hopefully Blinkly's mother can help us get to Taycod."

"Hold up! Follow me." Helmore led them to a table in the tavern's back corner. A man with tan skin, gold stud earrings, and colorful tattoos ate dinner. A tanned young girl sat beside him. "Captain Rahman," Helmore greeted the man, "my friends need a ship to Taycod. Could ya help them?"

"We leave for Malamox tomorrow morning. Taycod is on our way." Captain Rahman explained in a thick accent. "A silver bit will cover supplies if you're interested."

Blinkly reached for his pouch. "A silver bit is well worth not having to worry my mother."

Nate couldn't believe his fortune. He got to see one of his best friends and they'd still make it to Taycod after all. *So much for Thorton trying to stop me from becoming a wizard!*

Chapter Sixteen

THE QUEEN ALMARA

The morning sun colored the western horizon. Helmore, Nate, and Blinkly reached *The Queen Almara*. The fine, redwood sailing ship moored at the docks had an upper deck boasting three masts. The middle, largest mast supported a lofty crow's nest. The bow's figurehead was an intricately hand-carved bust of a beautiful yet fierce woman. A small cabin with an elegant redwood door at the stern served as the captain's quarters. A pair of identical staircases flanked the cabin door and led to the ship's helm.

"Thanks for arranging a way for us to get to Taycod and letting us stay the night, Helmore." Nate patted him on the shoulder.

"Glad I could help." Helmore grinned. "Just don't forget me when ya're a powerful wizard!"

"I won't," Nate promised. He followed Blinkly up the gangplank, calling over his shoulder, "I'll see you when I'm in the city again."

Captain Rahman greeted Nate and Blinkly when they stepped onto the ship. "Welcome aboard." He turned to the young woman who was dining with him the night before. "Noma, please get these young men settled below. I must prepare for departure."

"Of course, father." Noma gestured for Nate and Blinkly to follow. Rahman joined his crew.

Nate stared at a stout minotaur heaving supplies across the deck.

"That's Ahmin, our chef," Noma explained. She pointed to a pot-bellied, bald dwarf inspecting the sails. "Jorel is the first mate and that," she pointed to a young, fit dwarf coiling a rope, "is his nephew, Onar. This way, please." She opened a hatch near the front of the ship. "Watch your step and your heads."

Noma led Nate and Blinkly down a creaky ladder into the crew's quarters on the lower deck. Nate stooped under a low-hanging lantern. A pair of tiered hammocks stretched between two beams. Noma gestured to identical hammocks and a sea chest on the opposite wall.

"You'll sleep here. You can put your things in the chest. There are wool blankets in there if you need them."

"Thanks." Nate eyed the hammocks. The boat jerked. He took a step backward.

"We're pushing off," Noma said. "Let's get back on deck."

Bursting with anticipation, Nate and Blinkly stowed their packs. Nate followed Noma unsteadily back up the steep ladder.

A strong breeze filled the main sail and carried them past the ships in the harbor. Nate's eyes were wide. He grinned with excitement. The ship entered the Green Sea. Jorel and Onar raised the outer sails.

The Queen Almara cut briskly through the open water. Orange flying fish skimmed across the glistening waves. Nate began sweating. A pod of lilac dolphins played hide-and-seek in the ship's wake. Nate's stomach churned. In the distance, two white whales spouted water. Nate bolted for the ship's side and hurled.

Blinkly appeared by Nate's side.

Nate wiped his mouth with his sleeve. "What's wrong with me?"

"You're seasick. My first day on a ship was the same. Tomorrow should be better."

"I hope you're right."

By dinnertime, Nate's stomach was somewhat settled. A brilliant sunset lit the evening sky. The air was cooler. Nate joined Blinkly at the rear of the ship, marveling at the seemingly unending ocean.

"You're quite the sailor, Blinkly."

"You learn a thing or two when you're at sea for months on end. I'm glad you stopped vomiting."

They peered into the night sky. *The stars go on forever, even more than the sea. I wonder what else is out there.* Nate and Blinkly sat in silence. Nate was lost in his thoughts.

"It's a beautiful sight, isn't it?" Captain Rahman said. Nate and Blinkly jerked.

"It is," they agreed.

"The stars are essential to sea travel. You see that constellation?" Rahman pointed to a group of stars that appeared to form a jagged whip tapering to a point. "That's the Dragon's Tail. If we keep the tip of the tail in our sights, we know we're moving north. And that one," Rahman pointed to three exceptionally bright stars, "is known as the Sentry Eyes. It always points due east.

"Tomorrow night we will pass Taycod's port city, Wishington. Your escort party would have docked there today. Our smaller ship can go further up the coast, saving you about two day's journey on foot. When you reach the Crossroads Inn, the bar maiden will know if the escort party has passed.

"Use caution. King Tilus has chosen to stay neutral in the war. Bounty hunters throughout the kingdom are paid handsomely to kill or capture anyone associated with the Halls of Magic."

"Yes, sir." Nate tried to remember what he was learning. He was exhausted. "Thank you for everything."

Nate and Blinkly followed Onar to the crew's quarters. Nate spread a blanket from the sea chest on the floor. He caught Onar's eye. Onar stood with his arms across his chest.

"I think I'll do better on the floor," Nate insisted.

"Nonsense," Onar protested. "You'd be rolling all over the place. Knocking your head against the ship isn't going to make tomorrow any better."

Blinkly pointed to the top hammock. "After you."

Nate sighed. "I'll try."

Onar steadied the hammock. Nate climbed in. He was immediately pitched out. Bouncing off the lower hammock, he flopped onto the hard floor. Blinkly and Onar chuckled.

Nate crawled into the lower hammock. It wobbled. He lay on his back. It stopped. "I'm staying down here."

"Fair enough." Blinkly braced himself against the wall. With one push, he was snug in the upper hammock.

Exhaustion overtook Nate. He slipped off to sleep while Onar and Blinky talked about their love of sailing.

The next morning, Nate's stomach was only slightly queasy. Around mid-day, intense hollering from the crow's nest sent the crew into a frenzy. Nate and Blinkly couldn't understand Onar's native language. Captain Rahman exited his quarters. Nate and Blinkly darted toward him.

"Captain. What's happening?" Nate asked.

"Onar's spotted a fleet of Dread Vikings." Rahman rushed to Noma and Ahmin on the starboard side of the ship. "They're coming this direction. Hopefully our small ship won't be worth their time." He turned his attention to the helm. "Keep her steady, Jorel."

Moments later Nate gaped. Seven sleek, dark ships glided toward them several boot-lengths above the water on a misty, white haze. They weren't changing their course.

Rahman gave orders. "Jorel, turn into the wind. Ahmin and Blinkly, open the rest of the sails. Let's hope they tire of the chase."

Everyone scrambled. Nate rushed to help Blinkly. Once the wind filled the sails, the ship cut sharply through the waters. They watched anxiously. The Vikings pursued, bearing rapidly down on them.

"Ahmin, get the crossbows. Onar, get down here," Rahman commanded. "We can't outrun them. We'll have to fight. Noma, get below."

"You know me better than that, father." Noma snatched a crossbow from Ahmin when he returned. Ahmin distributed the remaining weapons. Nate pulled his wand from his boot.

"Don't let them board!" Rahman boomed. "Jorel, maneuver away from them."

Within moments, Nate caught his first glimpse of the fearsome beings. Outfitted in black leather armor and horned helmets, their pale skin and glowing red eyes chilled Nate's blood. With spears ready to attack, the warriors jeered threateningly toward *The Queen Almara.*

The Dread Vikings bombarded *The Queen Almara* with spears. The crew retaliated, releasing a wave of bolts from their crossbows. The battle continued. The crew dodged spears and occasionally connected their bolts with a warrior. One Viking was about to release his spear. Nate used his wand to entrap him in gooey blue slime. The Viking fell backward into the sea before the goo hardened. The Vikings drew closer.

"Blinkly," Nate yelled, "get the imagery potion!"

"Great idea!" Blinkly set down his crossbow. He blinked himself over to the front hatch and disappeared below. He returned with the imagery potion.

Three spears pegged into the outer planks of the ship next to Nate. Blinkly popped the bottle's cork. He flung the contents of the potion out into the water.

A massive, green sea serpent surfaced, shooting water straight into the air. Each of its eight vicious, scaly heads was easily the length of *The Queen Almara.* The heads lashed out in every direction, shrieking loudly and snapping their elongated fangs. The Viking ships swerved around the serpent. Two ships collided.

"Change course!" Rahman commanded.

Jorel steered *The Queen Almara* away from the battle scene. The Vikings didn't pursue them.

"Great imagination!" Nate slapped Blinkly.

"Well done, boys!" Rahman praised.

That night, the weather turned cold. A storm approached. Nate wrapped himself in a blanket on deck. They sailed past Wishington. He watched thousands of lights twinkle across the countryside. On a cloud high above the city, a sky castle sparkled. Nate was awestruck. *What else is this adventure going to bring?*

Chapter Seventeen

THE CROSSROADS INN

Three-stories high, the Crossroads Inn's decaying walls sagged. Warped extra-wide double doors hung crookedly on their rusty iron hinges. The roof's few remaining shingles quivered in the stiff wind. Broken shutters banged loudly.

A brisk wind scattered thick maple leaves from the surrounding forest across the yard. The barren trees trembled in the cold drizzle. Withered plants looked like mere shadows of their former selves. Weeds surrounding the front porch steps looked ready to attack.

Nate hesitated. Blinkly didn't. *Does he fear anything?* Nate shook his head. He followed Blinkly through the rickety double doors. The entire main floor was a tavern.

A group of olive-skinned peasants laughed, joked and sang, clearly enjoying their mugs of bubbler. They didn't speak Nate's language. It didn't even sound like Captain Rahman's language. A plump satyr sat passed out in a drunken stupor. His head hung off the table. Drool dripped from his gaping mouth into a pool of slobber on the floor.

Four colorful halflings dined merrily at another table. The female halfling's curly hair was partially covered by a bright-pink pointed hat that matched her ankle-length dress. The three male halfings wore brilliant blue tunics over lime-green stockings. Tight green caps were pulled snuggly over their ears.

I guess we're safe if the halfings aren't worried. Nate allowed his body to finally relax.

Stepping toward the bar, Nate noticed a young elf woman sitting alone. She glanced up. Tiny braids of lavender hair settled around her flawless, fair complexion. Nate gazed into her amethyst eyes. He felt a connection to her he couldn't explain. She smiled and returned to her meal. Her sleeveless golden armor revealed her shapely arms. The fancy darkwood bow over her shoulder drew his attention even more than the silly halflings.

She looked up again. "May I help you?"

"Ah . . . n-n-no," Nate stammered, realizing he'd been staring. Feeling his face going flush, he forced a smile and hurried to join Blinkly at the bar.

"We'll take two bowls." Blinkly told the bar maiden. He filled Nate in. "All they have is red pea gumbo."

"At least it's something." Nate was hungry.

"Any bubbler fer yeh? It's nice and thick."

"Do you have anything else?" Nate asked.

"Hollyapple juice er water."

"We'll try the hollyapple." Nate cocked his head at Blinkly.

Blinkly nodded in agreement.

The bar maiden set two wooden bowls full of steaming gumbo on the counter.

"Has an escort party from Versii passed by?" Nate asked.

"I already told yer friend," she scowled, filling two tin mugs with bright green juice. "No one's passed through here in three days. That'll be four bits."

Nate paid her. They carried their food to a table along the back wall.

"I guess I should've warned you I already asked," Blinkly chuckled. "She's not the friendliest person around."

"I noticed." Nate slurped a bite of gumbo. "Wait until Thorton sees that we beat him here. He's going to be mad!"

The female halfling approached Blinkly. She touched his shoulder. "Hello! I'm Mysty. My friends and I are in town picking up supplies for the Halls of Magic. I haven't seen you around here before."

"What a coincidence. We're also on our way to the Halls of Magic." Blinkly puffed out his chest.

Nate shot Blinkly a nasty glare. *Doesn't he remember Rahman's warning?*

"I'm Blinkly and this is Nate. He's a wizard in training."

"N-n-no, I'm not," Nate snapped. "He just likes to make up stories." He glared at Blinkly again.

"We love when new guests come to the Halls. I'll get the others so that you can meet them." She skipped back to her table.

"What are you doing?" Nate's heart pounded in his chest. "We're not supposed to tell people where we're going."

"Have you ever heard of a halfling bounty hunter?" Blinkly raised his eyebrow at Nate. "Relax. They're from the Halls. It'll be good to already have friends when we get there."

Nate slurped down another bite of gumbo, hoping it would settle the jitters in his stomach. The four halflings returned. Nate and Blinkly stood to greet them.

All three male halflings had pudgy noses that scrunched up when they grinned. The only difference between them was the color of their unfriendly eyes. Nate half-heartedly smiled back. The female's eyes looked cold. Nate didn't trust them.

"My full name is Mystria. This is Twin Blade, Iron Fist, and Double Claw."

Those don't sound like halfling names. Nate's stomach twisted in a knot.

"How'd you get names like those?" Blinkly's voice betrayed a hint of unease.

"Like this." Mystria removed her hat. It vanished. She grew from a halfling to a lanky, pale lady with long, blood-red hair. The sleeves of her red dress flared at her wrists. The hem brushed her knees. Her eyes bore the same dark coldness. Her dark-red lips sneered.

Nate and Blinkly stared in shock. Twin Blade removed his cap. He transformed into a muscular dwarf with a single long black tuft of hair protruding from the back of his head. He wore dark-grey chain mail armor. A tattoo of a ten-legged black spider with blood dripping from its

fangs covered his thick neck. Twin Blade pulled
two razor-sharp hatchets from the sheaths at his
waist.

In the same instant, Iron Fist and Double
Claw removed their caps. At his real height, Iron
Fist's steely grey eyes bore straight into Nate's.
Nate gasped. Iron Fist smirked through a full
black beard. His curly black hair hung down to
the shoulders of his spiked iron breastplate. He
held a spiked club in his right hand. His left hand
was a solid iron fist.

Double Claw stood several boot-lengths taller
than Nate. His bulky frame resembled a troll with
hairy ears and feet. In place of his hands, two
large metal claws kept snapping together.

Nate and Blinkly stepped back. Double Claw
clutched Nate around the neck with his right
claw. He lifted him high into the air. Nate pulled
his wand from his boot. Double Claw slammed
him up against the wall. The wand fell to the
floor.

"Let him go!" Blinkly threw his shoulder into
Double Claw's side.

Double Claw didn't even flinch. Blinkly bounced off Double Claw and tumbled over a chair. He landed in the unconscious satyr's drool.

Double Claw sneered.

The tavern patrons stampeded outside. Twin Blade strutted over to Blinkly and stepped on his chest.

"I'll have none of that in my tavern!" the bar maiden bellowed. She pulled a crossbow out from underneath her counter and aimed it at Mystria, "Git outta here now!"

Mystria scowled. She faced the bar maiden with her hands clasped. "Batista!" Mystria threw her hands open. A swarm of bats flew from her hands straight across the room toward the bar maiden.

The bar maiden stumbled backward. The crossbow flew from her hands. Striking her head against the wall, she slumped to the floor. The bats collided with the bar and evaporated. Mystria faced Nate.

"You don't look like a wizard." She picked up Nate's wand and rolled it in her fingers. Nate gasped for breath under Double Claws grip. "But we're paid just to stop you from reaching the Halls." She threw the wand out of Nate or Blinkly's reach. "Kill them!"

Tightening his grip, Double Claw leered coldly. Nate kicked frantically.

"Release them!" the purple-haired elf demanded from a table near the entrance. She was poised to attack.

"Your arrow is no match for me!" Mystria turned to the elf.

"Catch it, then!" The purple-haired elf released a white arrow.

Just before it struck her forehead, Mystria caught it in her right hand. She smirked.

The arrow stretched into a long silky thread, which swiftly enveloped Mystria's body. She was encased in a silky cocoon. The cocoon fell to the ground with a thud.

Nate stopped struggling against Double Claw's grasp. He felt dizzy.

The elf aimed a dark-blue arrow at Iron Fist. He pointed his iron fist at her. It detached from his arm and flew directly at her, striking her in the chest.

"Uh!" Falling backward, she hit her head on the table and collapsed.

Blinkly blinked out from underneath Twin Blade's foot. Twin Blade stumbled. Blinkly appeared next to Double Claw and sliced Double Claw's arm with his dagger. Cursing, Double Claw jerked back. His claw released Nate. Nate collapsed to the floor, gasping for breath.

Twin Blade charged, swinging his hatchets at Blinkly's head. Blinkly blinked onto a nearby table. Twin Blade lost his balance and crashed through the tavern's back wall.

"Now it's your turn!" Blinkly yelled at Iron Fist.

Iron Fist's fist circled back around. Nate tried to warn Blinkly, but couldn't speak.

Double Claw raised Nate into the air again.

The fist struck Blinkly in the back, knocking him off the table. Blinkly rocked on the floor. The fist reattached to Iron Fist's arm.

Nate gaped. He wished he'd picked up his wand.

Iron Fist strode over to Blinkly. Raising his spiked club over his head, he declared, "Time to die!"

"He won't die today!" An elf filled the doorway. His sleeveless gold breastplate emphasized his bulky biceps. His lavender hair was in a ponytail. Colorful arrows filled the quiver over his shoulder. His readied bow held three arrows—one dark red, one bright yellow, and one green.

"There's only one of you and three of us," Iron Fist sneered. Twin Blade crawled back through the wall. "Do you really think you can stop us?"

The elf released his arrows. Twin Blade and Iron Fist charged at him. Before they were halfway across the room, the first, red arrow exploded against one of Twin Blade's hatchets. The tavern shook violently. The blast made Nate's ears ring painfully. Twin Blade flew backward, creating another hole through the tavern's back wall.

The second, yellow arrow struck Iron Fist's metal fist. The resulting bolt of lightning entered his body and coursed through his entire frame.

His hair stood on end. He fell to the ground, shrieking and jerking uncontrollably.

Nate felt limp against the wall. Double Claw turned just when the third, green arrow reached him. He threw Nate to the side. Catching the arrow, he smugly snapped it in half and threw it to the ground. The arrow transformed into a small oak tree. Shooting up rapidly, it entangled Double Claw in its expanding branches. The branches carried Double Claw through the ceiling.

Nate wriggled in pain.

"Princess, Princess, are you okay?" The muscular elf rushed to the young elf's side. He scooped her motionless body into his arms and rushed out the door.

Blinkly snatched the healing potion from his pack and hurried to Nate's side. "Drink this." Blinkly slowly poured three drops into Nate's mouth.

Nate forced the hot liquid down. Once he swallowed, he could breathe easily again. The bruises and lacerations on his neck vanished.

"Wow! That stuff really works." Nate sat up. "We'd better give some to the others."

Nate grabbed his wand. The bar maiden sat slumped by the wall. They gave her three drops of potion before rushing outside to find the elves. The rain pounded the ground. The wind howled. The elves were nowhere to be seen.

"Where'd they go?" Blinkly looked around.

Nate scanned the area. *How'd they get out of here so quickly?*

"Get me down!" A voice carried on the wind.

Nate and Blinkly looked up. A massive oak tree stuck out of the Crossroads Inn's roof.

Trapped within the oak's branches, Double Claw flailed. "Did you hear me? Get me down!"

Walking backward, Nate pulled Blinkly's sleeve. He didn't want to take his eyes off Double Claw. "We'd better find the escort party."

Chapter Eighteen

TURNING BACK

Constant drizzle stung Nate's eyes, obscuring his vision. "Where's the escort party?" He fought against a gust of wind. "I figured we'd run into them by now."

Nate and Blinkly rounded a corner. A lifeless figure looked like a heap in the middle of the road. They exchanged concerned glances and drew closer. An extremely old, naked man lay in a pool of blood. He had suffered numerous deep wounds. His wrinkled skin was pasty white. The few patches of grey hair on his head were tangled masses of dirt and twigs.

"Heeelp meeeeeeee!" A shallow, desperate plea came from the old man's cracked lips. Nate and Blinkly jumped back.

"He's alive!" Nate exclaimed.

Pulling a light blanket from his knapsack, Blinkly gently covered the old man. Gingerly, Nate lifted his head. Blinkly dribbled three drops of the healing potion into his mouth. The old man attempted to spit out the hot liquid. Nate held his jaw shut until he swallowed. Instantly, his injuries began to heal. All signs of his wounds vanished.

"That's quite the stuff yeh have there, boys." The old man's tone was weak. Slowly, he sat up. "I think I need a little more."

"That's all you need," Blinkly assured him. The rain had already soaked through the blanket. The boys helped him to the shelter of a nearby tree.

"You were hurt pretty bad," Nate said. "It may take awhile for you to regain your full strength."

"Help me git outta here," the old man begged.

"What's the rush?" Nate asked.

"A vicious beast out there killed a whole band of soldiers. I fought it off 'n barely survived."

"Where are the soldiers' bodies?" Nate tried not to let his alarm show in his voice.

"We have ta git outta here."

"Where are the bodies?" Blinkly demanded.

"Back in those trees. Trust me, it's a sight yeh don't want ta see. Now get me out . . ."

Nate darted toward the trees. Blinkly blinked ahead. The old man's plea faded into the howling wind.

When Nate reached the clearing in the trees, there was no doubt it was the scene of a vicious attack. The war wagon, marred by long claw marks and gashes, lay on its side. Its door, dangling by one hinge, banged in the wind. Splintered wood and debris from the wagon littered the muddy terrain. Three torn, crippled tents had been thrown aside.

On the side of the clearing, the roots of several smaller trees were exposed, pushed to the ground in a crude path. Near the downed trees, two horses lay with fatal gashes to their sides. Ropes that had secured the other horses were slashed. They wafted fitfully in the wind.

"Over here, Nate," Blinkly yelled.

Nate rushed to Blinkly's side near the destroyed tents. Blinkly knelt over the bodies of two soldiers.

"We're too late." Blinkly was somber. "These two are already dead. We'd better search the camp. Hopefully someone survived."

Nate's gaze fixed on the dead soldiers. A blood-stained sword and a battered axe lay near them. Their helmets had been knocked to the ground. Their skulls were crushed.

Nate's stomach churned. His head spun the same way it had when he witnessed the massacre within the mural in Blinkly's room. He shook his head to clear his mind.

Brushing the rain from his eyes, Nate helped search the camp for survivors. Behind the broken tents, he heard a rustle and low moaning from the outlying underbrush. A leg protruded from the shrubs. A muscular, bald, black knight dressed only in leather pants lay face down. A deep gash on his back oozed blood. His only movement was a slight shudder when he groaned.

"Blinkly! I found someone alive!"

Blinkly appeared next to Nate. They carefully rolled him onto his back and gave him three drops of the healing potion.

The knight opened his eyes and stared in amazement. "I thought I was dead for sure." He struggled to stand. With Nate and Blinkly's help, he stumbled out of the bushes. As if forcing himself to ignore his weakened condition, he stood tall and brushed himself off. "My name is Haldon. Who are you boys?"

"I'm Danzandorian Gordenall and this is Nathanial McGray." Blinkly pointed first to himself, then to Nate. "We were supposed to join your escort party to the Halls of Magic but Thorton had you leave without us."

"If this is true, I would normally apologize but that may have been a blessing." Haldon surveyed the disastrous campsite. "Have you found any more survivors?"

"We've only found two dead soldiers and you," Nate reported.

"We better keep looking," Haldon insisted. "There were nine of us, including young Lord Brade. We'll probably find him under the war wagon. He ducked under there when the trouble started."

Nate ran over to the wagon and peeked underneath. He heard a soft whimper. He'd found Thorton.

"Help . . . me, I'm . . . dying," Thorton sniveled.

"Can you crawl out here?" Nate asked. Blinkly and Haldon arrived.

"I'm . . . too weak."

The three rescuers rolled their eyes. Nate grabbed one arm while Haldon grabbed the other. They easily pulled Thorton out.

"I think you boys can handle him from here. I'll keep looking for the others." Haldon began his own search.

"I'll help you look." Blinkly handed Nate the healing potion.

Nate examined Thorton for injuries. "You're lucky, Thorton. There's just a small scratch and it barely bled."

"Lucky?" Thorton yelled. "I'm sitting in the pouring rain with a wound that is going to kill me. How is that lucky?"

"Here, I'll give you some healing potion if you'll stop whining." Nate poured one drop into Thorton's mouth.

Thorton swallowed. He coughed and grabbed his throat. "I almost died once. Are you trying to kill me again?"

"Quit complaining," Nate insisted. "We need to help find other survivors."

"I can't." Thorton lay back down on the ground. "I'm still too weak."

"No, you're not. You were hardly even hurt. Get up!" Nate pulled on Thorton's arm. Thorton yanked his arm away and lay back down, folding his arms defiantly across his chest.

"Forget it," Nate said in disgust. "I'll go without you."

Blinkly waved Nate over. Out of the remaining five soldiers, two were dead and three were struggling for life.

"How did this all happen?" Nate gave some healing potion to the wounded.

"Just as we were bunking down for the night, a raging beast attacked us," Haldon explained. The soldiers' terrible injuries began to heal. "The soldiers on guard held it off. The rest of us grabbed our weapons. They were the first ones you found.

"You men," Haldon instructed the healed soldiers, "track down our horses. We need to move out."

"What happened to the beast?" Blinkly followed Nate and Haldon to the war wagon.

"It slumped out of camp mortally wounded, leaving us for dead. Fate was on our side. You showed up just in time."

"Sir," a soldier approached Haldon. "We found two horses."

Once the war wagon was repaired, the deceased were placed inside. Haldon gestured to two of the soldiers. "You will return to our ship and sail home with our four fallen comrades. The rest of us will continue our escort to the Halls of Magic on foot."

Thorton leaped to his feet in a sudden burst of energy. "I'm going back to Versii."

Nate stepped in front of him. "What are you talking about, Thorton? What about becoming a wizard? What about the war?"

"I don't care about the war." Thorton pulled himself up to the wagon seat. "I've been away from home for less than a week and was almost killed by a vicious beast. I'm going and you can't stop me."

Haldon turned to Nate. Nate stared dumbfounded at Thorton. "I'm sorry but our assignment is to escort young Lord Brade. This is his decision. We must see him safely home. You're welcome to join our party, but if you continue to the Halls, you'll be on your own."

"I didn't come this far to give up," Nate said. He looked at Blinkly. "Are you still with me?"

"Absolutely."

"The weather is starting to clear. Stay at the Crossroads Inn tonight," Haldon suggested.

"Don't tell anyone where you're going. This land is crawling with bounty hunters who will harm you if they know where you're headed."

Nate and Blinkly looked at each other and grinned.

"We found that out the hard way," Nate said. "I don't think we'll be welcome at the Crossroads Inn tonight."

A look of confusion crossed Haldon's face. "If you can't stay at the inn, you'd better build a fire big enough to keep the grimhounds away. We'll leave you with what little food we can spare. I'm afraid that's all we can do." With a sigh, Haldon put a hand on Blinkly and Nate's shoulders. "Stay on this road until you see the Halls. You should reach them by tomorrow evening. I admire your courageous determination."

Nate looked once more at Thorton. Thorton didn't meet his gaze. *I can't believe he'd just quit and leave us on our own like this!*

Chapter Nineteen

THE BEAST

Determined to avoid a repeat of their trouble at the tavern, Nate and Blinkly listened to Haldon's advice and travelled swiftly. They acknowledged other travelers with only courteous nods. When the sun started setting, they made camp in a clearing off the highway. Nate showed Blinkly how to scavenge for dry wood using tricks he'd learned from his father. Soon they had a blazing bonfire sure to ward off the grimhounds.

With the purple moon lighting the cold night, they basked in the warmth of the flames and shared a meager meal. Though exhausted, they agreed to stand guard together to keep each other awake. Their conversation slurred. Their eyelids drooped. By the time the orange moon peaked, they slept soundly.

Nate awoke with a start. "Did you hear something?"

A low rumble sounded from deep within the forest. They jumped to their feet. Blinkly grabbed a torch from the fading fire. Nate pulled his wand from his boot. He shivered. They faced the dark forest and listened. The rumbling grew louder and closer.

"That doesn't sound like grimhounds." Blinkly drew his dagger.

A fierce roar echoed through the forest. The trees shook violently. Snapping branches flew in every direction. One came right at Nate. He ducked to avoid being struck in the head. A monstrous beast burst into view.

On its hind legs, the fiend stood at least twice as tall as Nate. Covered from head to toe in thick fur, its huge, yellow eyes glowed. Its massive legs looked like tree trunks. Its bulging arms arched at the shoulders. Long, piercing claws protruded from its enormous paws. Its roar caused Nate's entire body to tremble with fear.

Lumbering toward them, the beast stopped at the fire. It crouched down on all four paws. Its claws churned the dirt. Eye level with Nate, the creature glowered at them over the flames. It grinned with a mouth full of razor-sharp teeth. The beast drooled from both corners of its mouth. Roaring so loud the leaves quivered, the brute shook its head, splattering saliva over Nate and Blinkly.

Run! Nate commanded himself. He stared into the monster's mouth. His limbs wouldn't respond. He heard a low mumble from Blinkly who seemed to be trying to talk to the beast. The beast swiped the dirt with its mighty paw, extinguishing half of the fire.

"Nate! The beast won't listen to me!"

Nate pointed his wand. His hand shook uncontrollably. "S-s-snare . . ."

The creature's eyes fixed on Nate. It roared again. The roar sounded like hideous laughter.

"You can do this," Blinkly encouraged. "Concentrate!"

Without breaking eye contact, the beast's paw smothered the remaining flames. The campsite darkened.

"Keep back." Blinkly thrust his torch at the beast. It backed away a few steps.

"Snare—E-e-e . . ." Nate stuttered. The wand did nothing.

"Nate! Snap out of it!" Blinkly yelled.

The mighty beast lunged. A red glare glinted from its teeth. Blinkly shoved Nate out of the way and disappeared.

Toppling to the hard ground, pain shot through Nate's shoulder, waking him from his fright. He spied the dwindling flames of the torch lying in the dirt. Nate grasped his aching shoulder. He tightened the grip on his wand.

He spun over onto his back. The beast towered above him on its hind legs. "Snare—Eran!"

The thick, dark-blue substance encircled the furry legs. The beast thrashed, tearing through the hardening muck. Throwing chunks of it in all directions, it broke free. It slashed at Nate with a powerful paw.

Nate rolled away. The creature's claws scraped the ground, spraying Nate with pebbles. Dropping to all fours, the beast gnashed its teeth to bite Nate.

Nate kicked the creature in the jaw with his heel. Throwing its head back, the beast roared. Nate clambered to his feet. He pointed his wand at the monster. Blinkly appeared in front of the beast.

"Blinkly! Get away!" Nate was ready to cast the spell.

Gripping his dagger, Blinkly drove it into the beast's stomach. It bellowed and lashed out, striking Blinkly in the head with its paw. Blinkly flew through the air, slammed against the trunk of a tree, and fell to the ground. He slumped over.

Nate burned with rage. "Snare—Eran!" he bellowed. The goo caught the beast's ankles. "Snare—Eran!" He trapped its knees.

The mighty creature crashed to the ground. It writhed against the substance. There was no escape.

As quickly as the goo rose, the beast transformed. Its body shrunk. Its thick hair shriveled. The razor-sharp claws and monstrous snout vanished. When the substance reached chest level, the creature was merely a worn-out, wrinkly old man.

"You!" Nate screamed. He stared in horror at the old man they had saved from certain death with the healing potion. "How could you?"

"I was created ta kill. Ya should've let me die." The old man's eyes seemed hollow. The dark-blue substance encircled the greying head and hardened.

"Blinkly, Blinkly! Did you see that?" Nate hurried to his friend still slumped over under the tree. He shook him gently. There was no response. Nate rushed to Blinkly's knapsack for the healing potion. "It was the old man. And after we saved him!" He fumbled with the cork and rolled Blinkly onto his back. Supporting his neck, Nate poured three drops into his mouth.

Blinkly remained motionless. The drops of potion dribbled out of his mouth. Fear rose inside Nate. He poured three more drops into his friend's mouth. This time he held Blinkly's mouth shut and tipped his head back. There was still no response. Nate took his hand from Blinkly's mouth. Some potion escaped between Blinkly's lips.

"Blinkly!" Nate wiped potion off Blinkly's face with his sleeve. "You have to drink this!"

He lifted Blinkly's head once more and emptied the remaining five drops of potion into his mouth. Holding Blinkly's head lower than his neck, Nate made sure the entire potion went down his throat. Blinkly remained limp and lifeless. A lump grew in Nate's own throat.

"Please, please, wake up Blinkly!" Nate pleaded.

Tears streamed down Nate's cheeks. He shook Blinkly harder, hoping to force the slightest glimpse of life. Blinkly wasn't waking. Nate sobbed and held his friend until his arms ached. He lowered Blinkly to the ground.

"NOOOOOOO!" Nate screamed into the dark sky, his fists clenched in anger. "Why him? It should have been me!"

A bolt of lightning shot through the blackness. A thunderous boom shook the trees around him. A light rain began to fall. Nate collapsed next to Blinkly's deceased body. The light rain became a downpour. Nate didn't care. Piercing rain drops soaked his clothing. The cold wind howled.

He heard a pack of grimhounds baying in the distance. The howling grew louder. The grimhounds were approaching. Heaving Blinkly onto his back, Nate started for the road. He lost his footing in the slippery mud and toppled to the ground. He stood again and raised Blinkly onto his back. Carrying his friend, he shuffled out of the clearing. Reaching the edge of the trees, Blinkly's weight made Nate's legs buckle. They tumbled to the ground once more.

While hoisting Blinkly a third time, Nate heard yelping close by. Knowing he couldn't outrun the grimhounds while carrying Blinkly, he made a desperate decision. He arranged Blinkly's body underneath two trees. Blinkly looked as if he were sleeping. Nate stepped back.

"I'm sorry, Blinkly," Nate choked. He pulled his wand from his boot. "I will come back for you. I promise!"

"Take the medallion." It was Blinkly's voice.

Nate looked at Blinkly. He remained motionless. A medallion, dangling from a chain around his neck, peeked out from Blinkly's tunic.

"Take the medallion." Blinkly's voice said again. Blinkly didn't move.

Am I losing my mind? Nate knelt beside Blinkly and lifted the medallion in his hand. Its face was a mighty war hammer—the handle engraved into the gold and the head a massive ruby.

"Take the medallion!" There was no mistaking Blinkly's voice. "It is entrusted into your care."

Hearing the grimhounds so close their snarling raised the hair on the back of his neck, Nate transferred the medallion to his own neck. He pointed his wand at Blinkly.

"S-s-sna. Snare—Er-r-r," Nate choked. "Snare—Eran." A protective tomb encrusted his

211

friend's body. Nate stood motionless, his tears flowing freely.

Branches snapped. Dozens of glowing green eyes approached him. Consumed by nightmarish rage, Nate fled. Sloshing through the mud, he ran faster than he thought possible. Distancing himself from the grimhounds, he slowed slightly but kept running. The rain subsided. He didn't care.

Nate ran until the sun appeared among the jagged peaks of the mountains in the west. He crested the top of a gentle hill, slipped in a mud puddle, and tumbled head over heel down the steep slope on the other side.

Too exhausted to stop himself, Nate rolled dizzily until he came to an upright seated position at the bottom of the slope. In the distance, the sun glistened off an astonishing structure. He had found the Halls of Magic.

Chapter Twenty

MASTER LOPERIAN

Nate's lungs burned, his clouded head throbbed. Every part of his body ached. Exhaustion washed over him. He lay on his side and closed his eyes. Memories of the previous night flooded his mind. Stung by the thought of losing Blinkly, Nate's eyes flew open. He struggled to his feet.

The muddy road forked. Taycod Highway continued straight, disappearing into a forest. A narrow, side path veered into a swaying meadow of yellowing grass. Nate plodded along the path toward the blue building that shimmered in the distance.

Wavy images appeared on the horizon. Four furry, elf-like creatures approached on snow cougars. Nate assumed it was a mirage. He didn't stop until the front gremlin pressed his spear on Nate's chest. Nate was too tired to be scared.

The gremlin glared and demanded something. Nate only heard high-pitched squeaking.

"I don't understand." Nate shook his head.

The leader barked at the other three gremlins. They surrounded Nate with their cougars. The leader gestured for Nate to climb on the back of one of the huge cats. He mounted numbly. The cougars bounded away. Nate flopped from side to side. He forced himself to hold tightly to the saddle. They neared the Halls of Magic. Nate's mouth dropped.

The Halls were constructed entirely of sparkling, dark-blue crystal. A massive six-sided building was surrounded by twelve smaller towers of the same shape. The towers were connected to the center building by dozens of enclosed hallways. From the top of each tower, clear waterfalls filled a wide moat below.

On the bank of the moat, the gremlins halted in front of a simple wooden hut. Their leader dismounted and gestured for Nate to follow him inside. Sliding off, Nate glanced around nervously. The remaining gremlins had dismounted and stood behind him with spears readied. Nate slowly stepped inside.

The hut's interior was plain. A middle-aged, green-haired lady elf sat at a desk. She greeted Nate in a language different from the gremlin. Nate shrugged his shoulders. She smiled and pulled something out of the top drawer. Walking over to him, she slipped a ring onto his finger.

"Is that better?" she asked kindly.

To his surprise, he could now understand her perfectly. "Yes, much." He studied the small pink gem within the ring. "What is this?"

"It's an Idiom Talisman," she explained. "As long as you wear it you can communicate in all languages."

"What is your name?" In a gruff, yet high-pitched voice, the gremlin leader interrupted.

"I'm Nathanial McGray."

"Show me your identification parchment," the gremlin demanded.

"I . . . I don't have it. My pack was stolen."

The elf held up her hand. "That will do, Captain Galo. We are expecting a Nathanial McGray. Please leave us."

Glaring up at Nate, Galo stormed out of the hut.

"Please forgive his rudeness. With the on-going war we must be cautious. I'm Marian. Where is the rest of your party?"

"Thorton Brade returned home with the escort party and . . . and Blinkly, I mean Danzandorian is . . ." Nate struggled to finish. Tears escaped down his face, "is dead."

"Dead?" Marian gasped.

Nate nodded, wiping his cheeks with his sleeve.

"We must inform Master Loperian at once."
Marian led Nate into a tiny room with a full-
length mirror centered on the back wall. She
touched the mirror. The glass began to shimmer.

She grasped Nate's hand. "Come with me."
They stepped through the mirror and entered one
of the enclosed hallways. The walls were dark-
blue crystal. The floors were shiny chocolate-oak.
The inner walls were divided by oversized wooden
doors. She dropped his hand.

Nate looked over his shoulder. A full-length
mirror identical to the one in the hut ceased
shimmering. "How did we do that?"

"The Halls are full of magic," she replied.
"Think of where you need to go while you touch
the mirror. When it shimmers, step through."

Nate followed Marian in wonderment. The
transparent outer walls revealed a gremlin
patrolling the skies on the back of a brilliant
griffin. With glistening wings spanning several
boot-lengths, the majestic creature swooped along
the arches of the dazzling waterfalls.

"Nathanial, please keep up," Marian hurried
him along.

Nate realized he was dawdling. They rounded a corner. An inner wall cut across the hallway. Marian rapped on the lone door. It opened by itself, closing after they entered.

Landscape murals covered the walls. Lush chairs were tucked under small tables. The center support of the room was a circular bookcase. It stretched from the floor to the ceiling and held thousands of books.

Nate and Marian rounded the bookcase. A gentleman with wavy grey hair and olive skin sat behind a desk covered with strange trinkets. Laying a quill down on an open book, he pushed his spectacles up the bridge of his nose. To Nate's surprise, he moved with the stride of a much younger man when he rounded the desk to greet them.

"And who may this be?" He smiled kindly.

"Master Loperian, this is Nathanial McGray. I'm afraid he has terrible news," Marian said.

"What's that?" Master Loperian placed his hand on Nate's shoulder.

"Blinkly . . . Danzandorian is . . . dead," Nate sputtered, looking down at the ground and struggling to hold back tears.

"I'm sorry to hear that." Master Loperian waved Marian away. "Nathanial, you must tell the Red Wizard and me everything that happened."

"Yes, sir," Nate agreed. "Master Loperian, is there any magic that can bring Blinkly back to life?"

Master Loperian retrieved a worn wooden staff from behind his desk. "I wish it were possible but that is beyond any wizard's ability." He moved to a table that matched the seer stone Nate had seen in the Red Wizard's tower. "Have a seat."

Remaining standing, Master Loperian closed his eyes, held his staff out in front of him, and chanted softly, "Lamra—Hira—Istifia."

To Nate, nothing seemed to happen. Master Loperian lowered his staff to the floor and moved his lips silently. He opened his eyes and took the seat across from Nate.

"I just spoke with Dontrud. He's returning to his tower so we can visit through the seer stone," Master Loperian explained.

"Dontrud?"

"Oh, yes," he chuckled. "I usually refer to him as the Red Wizard to others but sometimes old habits break through."

The milky stone began to swirl. Leaning over the table, Nate stared into the face of the Red Wizard.

"Nathanial, is it true that Danzandorian is dead?"

"It's true."

The Red Wizard's forehead wrinkled. "I'm so sorry to hear that. How did it happen?"

Nate took a couple of deep breaths. "Thorton left us at the docks. We were robbed in the Crimson City and lost the invisibility potion. We crossed the Green Sea on *The Queen Almara* and used the imagery potion to scare away the Dread Vikings."

Nate stood and paced, gesturing while he spoke. The wizards only interrupted to ask for more details. They seemed to take great interest in the boys' rescuers at The Crossroads Inn.

Nate told of healing the old man and trying to save the escort party. He tried to hide his

resentment about Thorton's decision to go back
home but spoke well of Haldon. He recounted the
beast's attack and shook with anger when he
explained that the beast turned out to be the
same old man they saved earlier. He couldn't hold
back his tears.

He wiped his eyes. "I tried to bring him here
but I had to leave him behind to escape the
grimhounds. I used my wand to cover his body
for protection and ran until the sun rose."

Finishing his story, Nate realized he'd almost
forgotten about the wizards listening to him. He
let out a sigh and slumped back down into his
chair.

"I'm so sorry, Nathanial. I knew the journey
could be dangerous but I never imagined all the
tragedy that would happen," the Red Wizard
spoke from within the seer stone. "I must speak
to Lady Gordenall at once. I will be in touch." The
Red Wizard disappeared. The milky stone settled.

"Nathanial, you look deep in thought," Master
Loperian said.

"Yes, sir, I . . . I don't know if I belong here.
Maybe I should go home with Blinkly's body."

Master Loperian placed his hand on Nate's shoulder. "You've experienced a terrible tragedy. You're hungry and exhausted. Now is not the time to make drastic decisions." Reaching for his staff he continued, "We have some time before we send Danzandorian home. There is a story I'd like you to read. If you still want to leave after you have finished it, I'll respect your wishes. Does that sound fair?"

"Yes, sir."

Following Master Loperian toward the giant circular book case, Nate expected him to hand him a book. The wizard lifted his staff and said, "Danfor—Jasi—Mala."

The bookcase split down the middle. Nate was surprised when it opened to a giant mirror three times larger than the ones Nate had seen earlier that day. Master Loperian gently touched the glass.

Nate followed him through the shimmering mirror into a dank, gloomy cavern.

Chapter Twenty-One

GALAFADE THE GRAND

Engulfed by cool, moist air, Nate shivered. "Where are we?"

"This is the Oracle's Grotto." Master Loperian smiled reassuringly. He led Nate through the dim, torch-lit passageway.

They ventured deeper, passing bubbling pools, thick pillars, and jagged stalagmites. Just as

Nate's eyes began to adjust to the sparse lighting, a bright glow appeared in the distance. When they reached the end of the passageway, the source of the shine was revealed—two massive golden doors. At least twice as tall as Nate and equally wide, they were engraved with astrological symbols.

Hunched over, a pair of grey stone gargoyles crouched on each side of the doors, their wings folded loosely behind their backs. The gargoyle on the left held a massive sword. The one on the right held a giant mace. The glow of the doors cast long shadows over their bat-like faces, giving them a foreboding expression.

"Are they watching us?" Nate whispered, afraid to speak too loud.

"Of course, they're the guardians," Master Loperian explained. "But, you have nothing to fear if your heart holds no evil intent."

Placing his hand nervously over his heart, Nate stared up at the gargoyles. Master Loperian gently tapped the doors with his staff. To Nate's relief, the giant doors creaked open and they stepped safely inside a spacious, circular room.

From floor to ceiling, the shelves lining the walls were divided into slots. Most contained neatly rolled parchments. The parchments varied in color, creating a rainbow effect around the room. A wisp of a woman sat at a half circle desk writing on a golden scroll.

Without acknowledging her visitors, she stopped writing, rolled up the parchment, and placed it carefully next to six other differently colored scrolls on the desk. When the woman rose from her chair, Nate realized why she seemed so fragile. He could see right through her! Floating over to Nate and Master Loperian, she greeted them with a nod. She looked deeply into Nate's eyes. He felt like she could read his thoughts. Smiling gently, she vanished.

"What happened to her?" Nate looked around in surprise.

"I don't know. I don't fully understand all the mysteries surrounding oracles."

"So what is an oracle?"

"A magical being who records the history of Zndaria." Master Loperian motioned at the shelves of scrolls. "There is much we can learn from the trials or triumphs of others." He waved his staff in the air and chanted, "Alfa—Atafa—Darna." A bronze scroll floated off a far shelf and landed in his hand.

"This is one of my favorite stories. I hope you enjoy it after you've had some time to rest." He handed the scroll to Nate.

They returned to Master Loperian's office. Marian was waiting for them. She took Nate to his bedroom on a different floor.

Stepping into the room, Nate was astonished. The bed jutted into the room as if it were an extension of the wall. It held a feather mattress twice the size of Nate's at home. Its deep-red fluffy quilt made Nate want to dive in and go to sleep.

"This is your spindalier." Marian gestured to a brightly-lit crystal sphere hovering over a nightstand. It filled the room with light. "The spinning creates the glow. To darken your room, stop it with a touch. Another gentle touch will restart the rotation and the light will return.

Marian pointed to the desk where a clear cylinder orbited by a brass ring contained weather icons suspended in a clear liquid. "The diomiter displays the time of day and the current weather. Is there anything else you need right now?"

Nate glanced around the room. There was a wooden chair and several well-worn books on the desk. An assortment of colorful breads surrounded a pot of bubbling cheese. A three-shelf bookcase awaited Nate's belongings. He looked through an opening of an adjoining room where, to his surprise, an indoor outhouse was complete with a bathing pool and wash basin.

"I can't think of anything else I need, thank you." Nate saw her to the door.

He was starving. Dipping bread in the delicious cherry cheese, he didn't stop eating until it was all gone. He readied himself for bed and then lay down, scroll in hand, curious about Master Loperian's favorite story. He tried to read but realized how deeply tired he was. He laid the scroll on the nightstand and drifted off to sleep.

Awakened by a nightmare of the beast's attack, Nate jolted upright in bed. "Blinkly!"

From the light of the spindalier, Nate read the position of the orange and red moons on the

diomiter's brass ring. It was still the middle of the
night. Lying back down, he stared at the ceiling.
He wasn't falling back asleep. He picked up the
scroll and was soon lost in the story.

*When a satyr named Galafade was eight years
old, the deranged sorceress, Antipa, and her
ghostly blood banshees viciously attacked his
village in the Frozen Desert. They left everyone,
including his family, for dead. A band of desert
elves happened upon the village shortly after the
assault. Finding Galafade alive, pinned under a
fallen camel, the elves brought him to the Oasis
Fortress to be raised in their culture.*

*Over the next year, Antipa conquered the
Frozen Desert. Villages such as the Oasis Fortress
that accepted her rule with little resistance were
spared. All others faced the same fate as
Galafade's friends and family. Galafade matured
and was driven to rebellion.*

*One day, Galafade spoke with a shopkeeper.
"I'm sure that if we join together, Antipa can be
defeated!"*

"Hold your tongue!" The shopkeeper demanded. "If Antipa learns of your rebellion, you will be killed. I want no part in it."

Within a week, Antipa marched into the Oasis Fortress' town square with a battalion of banshees. Her orange, spiked hair and pasty complexion added to her menacing look.

"My spies tell me there is a rebel amongst you," Antipa declared to the assembled townsfolk. "Bring Galafade to me or you'll be destroyed!"

Fearful townsfolk dragged Galafade toward her.

Antipa cackled with delight.

"Don't do this!" Galafade pled.

The crowd said nothing. The deliverers shoved Galafade into the town square. Cowardly, they vanished into the masses.

"You are guilty of treason!" Antipa ordered her banshees to surround Galafade. "Your sentence is death! Asa—Esta! Asa—Esta! Asa—Esta!"

A green vapor steamed from the crystal orb atop Antipa's staff, encircling Galafade. He collapsed, struggling for breath. Antipa laughed. Just when death seemed certain, Antipa chanted *again. The green mist dissipated. Galafade labored to his feet.*

"If you wish to live," Antipa proclaimed, "bow before me and declare your unending loyalty!"

Standing taller, Galafade stared up into Antipa's dark-orange eyes. "I will never bow before you nor can I be guilty of treason. You are not the rightful queen!"

Antipa struck Galafade across his cheek. A nasty red welt swelled. "Death to the traitor! Banshees attack!"

Falling on their victim with brutal swipes of their razor-sharp nails, Galafade was struck down.

"NO!" Nate hurled the scroll across his room. Staring at the tangled scroll lying on the floor near the desk, he seethed. *How am I supposed to learn anything from him if he's dead!* Nate wiped sweat from his brow. His anger lessened. He wanted to know how the story ended. Sliding off the bed, he picked up the scroll and found his place.

"Let this be a lesson to you all," Antipa declared, "this fate awaits any who dare to defy me!"

That night, the elves buried Galafade. Their shame was almost unbearable. They had stood by, doing nothing as the most courageous of their own was murdered.

Word quickly spread of the young satyr who had bravely stood against Queen Antipa. Anger replaced their shame. It sparked courage in the inhabitants of the Frozen Desert.

Over the next year, tribes of desert elves, sand dwellers, nomad dwarfs, lizard men, and satyrs joined forces. They fought valiantly under the banner of Galafade. The war was long and bloody. Antipa was defeated. Peace was restored. A statue was erected in the Oasis Fortress town square. The plaque read:

Not all who die, die in vain!
United forever in remembrance of
Galafade the Grand.

I get it! Lying back down, Nate realized the deeper meaning of Galafade's story. *Blinkly did not die in vain,* Nate promised himself. *I will live my life to honor his death.*

Chapter Twenty-Two

APPRENTICES

Dear Lady Gordenall,

I am so sorry for what happened to Blinkly. He was a great friend. I wished I'd cast my spell sooner and saved him. After he died, I thought I heard his voice tell me to take his medallion. I will give it to you personally when I return to Burrowville after I finish at the Halls.

I've thought about coming home early but have decided to stay. I want to finish what I started with Blinkly. He would want that and I hope you feel the same. I promise to do my best to honor him.

Again, I am very sorry for Blinkly's death. I wish I could change the past. Blinkly was very brave and I hope to live in a way that is worthy of his sacrifice.

Forever in debt,

Nathanial McGray

Clutching the parchment, Nate stood with Master Loperian at the edge of a small clearing. In the chilly air, Nate watched somberly. A ghostly hand billowed from Master Loperian's staff. It peeled away Blinkly's crusty tomb.

Several gremlins reverently placed Blinkly's body into a crystal coffin. The setting sun shone brilliantly off the casket when the gremlins lifted it into the back of a heavily fortified war wagon.

Nate felt a loss for his friend but was at peace with his decision to stay.

Nate handed his parchment to a gremlin seated at the head of the wagon. "Please ask the soldiers on the warship to deliver this to Lady Gordenall."

"Yes, sir," the gremlin replied.

Nate stepped back. The gremlin snapped the reins on two ginormous wooly rams whose curled horns jutted a few boot-lengths above the wagon. The wagon slowly pulled out of sight.

Master Loperian took hold of Nate's elbow. "You've had a long day, Nathanial. It's time we get back. Al—May—Bestafy."

Nate appeared with Master Loperian outside his room at the Halls and stumbled slightly.

Master Loperian steadied Nate. "Get some sleep tonight. Tomorrow we begin your studies."

"Yes, sir."

Master Loperian disappeared. Nate entered his room, prepared for bed, and fell asleep as soon as his head hit the pillow. He slept soundly, waking well-rested early the next morning. He'd just finished dressing when there was a knock on his door.

Swinging the door open, Nate was greeted by a handsome young black man who appeared to be in his early twenties. Slightly taller than Nate, he had a thin build and silky black hair that draped past his shoulders. Dressed in a flowing deep purple robe, embroidered with elaborate gold thread, and a matching cap, he stood with relaxed confidence.

"Nathanial?"

"Yes, I'm Nate."

"I'm Sadaki and this is Bylo." Sadaki gestured to the shorter young man next to him. The hood of Bylo's coarse, forest-green robe lay on his back. His head was shaved.

"Please accompany us to breakfast," Bylo invited.

"Sure," Nate smiled, hungry and grateful for the offer.

Outside the transparent crystal walls, dark clouds blanketed the sky. A fluffy snow wafted down, dusting the ground. In the absence of sunshine, the walkway was illuminated by a mysterious radiance that cast playful shadows around the trio as they strolled and chatted about their families.

Sadaki was the son of a valiant witch doctor whose healing powers had saved thousands of their tribal members. Bylo's mother was a druid empress whose family had ruled benevolently over their clan for more than three hundred years.

"Tell us about your family, Nate," Sadaki insisted.

"Well, my family," Nate hesitated, "isn't exactly nobility."

"I told you!" Sadaki slapped Bylo on the back. "There've been rumors of a peasant coming from Versii to study with Master Loperian. Not everyone is happy about it but we think it's great."

"Really?"

"Indubitably," Bylo chimed in. "It's refreshing to see someone defeat our antiquated social constraints. Many of the nobles I know are dreadfully obtuse."

Nate looked to Sadaki with confusion.

"He means change is a good thing and not all nobles are as smart as they think they are."

They reached a full-length mirror and stepped through into a vast, yet sparsely filled, dining hall. With footsteps echoing against the granite floor, the trio passed several empty pedestal tables before taking their seats near the front of the hall.

"Have you acquainted yourself with the other mentors yet?" Bylo nodded toward a table at the head of the room where Master Loperian and other distinguished-looking individuals dined.

Nate shook his head.

"The illustrious couple adjacent to Master Loperian is the Kilnipy's." Bylo gestured to a picture-perfect couple. She wore a tailored, turquoise suit. His fine leather jerkin sported dozens of tiny leather pouches.

Nate nodded. *Illustrious must mean fancy.* He didn't want to ask about every word Bylo said. A gaseous cloud drifted to the mentors' table. It solidified into a solid-ice sculpture. Nate gaped. "What is that?"

"That's Ei," Sadaki chuckled. "He's an elementor. He can transform into any element and rarely looks the same two days in a row."

A young olive-skinned halfling arrived at Nate's table serving a platter of colorful dried fruit, miniature muffins, and black herbal tea. Nate thanked her and joined Sadaki and Bylo in filling their plates. They ate without talking for a few moments until Nate broke the silence.

"So, Sadaki. Who's your mentor?" Nate asked.

"We have the same teacher. I've been studying with Master Loperian for the past three years." Sadaki took another bite of fruit.

"What about you, Bylo?"

"Ms. Perrymire, the elf clothed in the green frock." Bylo motioned toward a plump brunette at the front table. "For the past twenty-two months, she's helped refine my aptitude in the art of summoning."

"Is everyone else an apprentice?" Nate gestured to the handful of individuals scattered throughout the room.

"Most of them, but a few are visitors who have come here to hone their skills. Some study for a few days; others stay for months," Sadaki explained. "Last year the entire room was full, but we've had fewer guests since the war began. If you're almost finished eating," he added, "Master Loperian asked us to give you a tour before you meet him in the Hall of Wizardry."

"That'd be great." Nate popped his last muffin into his mouth.

The trio cleared their plates and carried them to a crystal bin near the entrance. Stepping through the mirror, they entered the bottom level of the Halls—a spacious indoor garden.

This must be the garden Blinkly told me about. Nate followed Sadaki and Bylo along a cobblestone path winding through lush grass. Marble benches dotted the surroundings. Miniature trees blooming with brilliant saffron flowers filled the air with an alluring fragrance.

The only visitors in the garden were a woman and her two young daughters. Light-blue skin highlighted their gills and webbed hands and feet. Smooth, colorful suits fit snugly from their necks to the middle of their thighs. They splashed playfully in a crystal-green stream that babbled through the garden, emptying into a pool.

On an island in the midst of the pool, three life-size statues—a stately halfling holding a glimmering scepter, a white centaur playing a golden violin, and a handsome black woman holding a crystal staff—formed a triangle. The sculptures rotated slowly, encircled by a hovering banner that read:

Increasing our wisdom through embracing our differences.

"Hundreds of years ago, these three," Sadaki gestured to the statues, "wanted a place to study magic while learning from others. They created the Halls of Magic. Since then, the Halls have continually expanded. Each corridor extending from the center building to one of the smaller surrounding towers houses a form of magic. Nearly all forms of magic can be studied here."

"We resume our excursion through the different halls." Bylo led them away from the pool.

Through a full-length mirror, they entered a wide hallway.

Numerous brass chandeliers bore candles flickering with brilliant green flames. Blackwood bookcases and shelves held everything from dragon lice, fish eyes, and goblin hair to fairy tears, eel teeth, and boar tongues.

"What is all this?" Nate cringed.

"Ingredients," Sadaki explained. "Watch Aufila."

A young dark-skinned lady stood next to a purple book propped open on an easel crafted from a dragon's claw. Stirring the contents of a small black cauldron, she dropped what appeared to be a silver bat into the pot. Adding a pinch of white powder, she stepped away. A ghostly phoenix emerged from the cauldron, its wings spread widely, talons poised to attack. The corners of her mouth turned up proudly.

"Superlative, Aufila," Bylo commended.

"Thank you," she smiled. With a nod toward Nate she asked, "Who's this?"

"I introduce you to Master Loperian's newest apprentice, Nathanial McGray," Bylo said.

Aufila's smile disappeared.

Nate nodded.

Aufila waved her hand through the phoenix. It vanished. "Peasants don't belong here." She flung her wavy, dark hair over her shoulder and stormed off.

Nate was dumbfounded. His face blazed. *She doesn't even know me!*

"Don't let her get to you." Sadaki blew out a heavy breath.

"It's incredulous!" Bylo matched Sadaki's irritation. "Your birth status doesn't determine your propensity."

Nate was pretty sure he agreed with Bylo, but that didn't help his confidence. His shoulder's sagged.

"Aufilo and the others will come around as you prove yourself." Sadaki sounded positive. "Let's keep moving. We have a lot more to show you."

Bylo and Sadaki showed Nate many other Halls before leaving him in the Hall of Wizardry late in the afternoon.

Master Loperian greeted Nate. "How was your tour?"

"I had no idea there were so many forms of magic!" Nate gushed.

"I hope everyone made you feel welcome." Master Loperian ushered Nate further into the tranquil hall. Plush armchairs sat beside decorative six-sided tables. Fine mahogany bookcases lined the walls. The room was lit to the ideal brightness for reading. The temperature was comfortable.

"Sadaki and Bylo were great. Almost everyone else was nice, but," Nate hesitated, "it's obvious a few don't think I belong here."

"I'm afraid that is to be expected," Master Loperian consoled. "You're breaking tradition and that's difficult for some to accept. Give it time. Prejudice is best overcome through unwavering resolve."

"I'll remember that." Nate tried to sound optimistic. He noticed an enormous leather-bound book on a podium. "What's this?"

"It's *Sofyra's Collection.* She was one of the founders of the Halls of Magic. You should have seen her statue in the garden at the beginning of your tour."

Nate nodded.

"She filled this book with invaluable spells and knowledge that could have been lost forever. She was the first wizard to record this," he opened the book and gestured to a page filled with unique symbols, "the wizardry alphabet. It is the foundation of your training and must be mastered in order to progress. I suggest you find a comfortable seat." Master Loperian smiled. "It could be a long winter."

Nate stared at the symbols. This was it. He was finally going to learn magic!

Chapter Twenty-Three

LORETTA

Nathanial.

Nate sat up abruptly. Several parchments fell off his chest.

Nathanial?

Groggy, Nate answered telepathically. "Yes, Master Loperian?"

I need to see you before breakfast. Please come to my office.

"Yes, sir."

Gathering the scattered parchments, Nate realized he'd once again fallen asleep reading the letters he'd received over the winter months. He stacked them on his nightstand. One had fallen to the floor. Although he had it memorized, he scanned it briefly and placed it with the others.

Dear Nathanial,

Thank you for your touching letter. I appreciate knowing that my son was valiant to the end. Please don't consume yourself with guilt, you did your best. I agree that you should continue your studies and expect you to excel.

I wasn't aware that Danzandorian had a medallion but I am curious to see it when you return. Until then, please keep yourself safe.

With warmest regards,

Lady Gordenall

Nate dressed quickly, ran wet fingers through his shoulder-length hair, and headed to Master Loperian's office.

Rounding the circular bookcase, he asked, "You wanted to see me?"

"Yes, Nathanial, please sit down." Master Loperian motioned to the chair across from him. "I'm sorry to summon you so early. There is news from Versii." Master Loperian moved out from behind his desk into the seat next to Nate. A somber look crossed his face. "Yesterday, King Siddon's forces launched a surprise attack on the Northern Fort."

Nate reacted to the despair in Master Loperian's eyes. "How bad was it?"

"Alas, it was a swift and bloody battle. The heavy fortifications did nothing to stop the bloodthirsty horde. Before the night fell, most of the battalion had been slaughtered, including General Triatun."

Dread washed over Nate. *What about Ted?*

Master Loperian continued quickly as if responding to the sickened look on Nate's face.

"Your brother is alive. He is with those retreating to Burrowville."

Nate sighed with relief, but he was confused. "Don't we have spies or something so surprise attacks don't happen?"

"Our scouts had been watching for the army to approach swiftly but openly, as Siddon had attacked other countries. Unbeknownst to us until now, the Infinite Wizard has joined Siddon's army. Using a spell, he placed a mirage around their forces. It prevented us from seeing them until the morning of the attack."

"The Infinite Wizard?"

"Yes, someone the Red Wizard and I used to love very much." Master Loperian's eyes flickered with pain. "He betrayed us long ago, but we had heard nothing of him for the past several years. Foolishly, we assumed he was dead. Now that we're aware of him, we will be ready for the next attack."

Nate sat forward. "I want to be there for my family if the army attacks Burrowville. What can I do to help?"

"You can study even harder." Master Loperian patted Nate's shoulder. "You've come far over the last few months and have made commendable progress in overcoming your stuttering. The more you study, the more useful you will be. I will only allow you to go if you will assist, not impede, the Red Wizard's defenses."

"I'll be ready."

"Good," Master Loperian's tone lightened. "Because spring is finally here, and to help you further your training, we're going to the Black Stone Mountains this morning."

"We're leaving the Halls?" Nate nearly leaped to his feet.

"Yes." Master Loperian smiled at Nate's sudden enthusiasm. "I'll send Sadaki for you when it's time."

After breakfast, Nate retreated to his favorite armchair in the Hall of Wizardry. Half-heartedly, he flipped through the book on his lap. The foreign jargon finally seemed familiar to him, but studying was the last thing on his mind.

Sadaki suddenly appeared next to him dressed in a lightweight-wool cloak. "Are you ready?"

"Very." Nate grabbed his jerkin off the back of the chair.

"Okay, hold on to my arm and be quiet."

Nate did as he was told.

Sadaki shut his eyes tightly and crinkled his nose as if he were in pain.

Nate held back a laugh.

"Al—May—Bestafy."

Instantly appearing in the mountains, they tumbled to their hands and knees in black dirt.

"Sorry about that." Sadaki pulled himself to his feet and helped Nate stand.

Dusting off his knees, Nate marveled at the beauty of their surroundings. The knotty branches of thousands of enormous, twisted trees circled from the ground to the upmost leaves. They were covered with delicate purple blossoms. "It beats hiking up here."

"Yes. That'd take a couple of days." Sadaki pointed through a gap in the mountain at what appeared to be a miniaturized model of the Halls.

"Where's Master Loperian?" Nate glanced around them.

"Right here." Master Loperian and a lovely stranger appeared next to Nate as smoothly as if they'd been standing there all along. The stranger's alluring, black eyes met Nate's. "Nathanial, this is my granddaughter, Loretta."

Flashing a flawless smile, Loretta nodded at Nate. With olive skin and silky, black hair, she was a vision of beauty in a fitted light-green tunic, matching trousers, and flowing overcoat. Nate returned her nod with a clumsy smile.

"Loretta is an accomplished musician." Master Loperian beamed proudly. "She comes here to study every spring and can outplay nearly any musician I know."

"Grandfather, please," Loretta protested, "you're embarrassing me."

Captivated by her beauty, Nate watched the loving exchange.

"Of course I am, dear. That's one of the perks of being a grandfather." Master Loperian turned his attention to Nate. "Well, Nathanial. Are you ready to make your staff?"

"My staff? Of course!"

"The best staffs are made from the wood of these warped willows." Master Loperian pointed at the deformed trees in the dell. "You need a branch that is almost straight. It should be about half a boot-length taller than you. Loretta will help you search for a branch while Sadaki and I continue his training nearby."

"Perfect!" Nate exclaimed, hoping he didn't sound too eager.

"We'll meet back here at lunchtime. If you need us sooner, Loretta will call on her flute," Master Loperian said. "Do either of you have any questions?"

Nate and Loretta shook their heads.

"Very well. Lameria—Alama—Distafay!" With a low poof, a small cloud appeared under Master Loperian. He pointed his staff upward. The cloud rose, lifting him high into the air.

"Lameria—Alama—Distakay!" Sadaki followed Master Loperian's lead. Nothing happened.

"It's Dista*fay*!" Master Loperian instructed from above. "Try it again."

"Lameria—Alama—Distafay!" Sadaki's second attempt created a small cloud beneath him. He lifted his staff in the air and, wobbling, floated to catch up to Master Loperian. They drifted away.

"Are you ready?" Loretta asked.

"Sure." Nate had to concentrate extra hard to avoid stuttering. The anxiety he usually had around girls was mild compared to how he felt right now. His heart pounded and his sweat glands were in overdrive. Trying to sound witty, he eyed the forest and asked, "Do you think there's a straight branch in here?"

"Of course there is," Loretta insisted, adding with a touch of humor in her voice, "but we should get started in case it takes a while to find."

After they searched for a couple of hours, Nate felt completely comfortable around Loretta.

She pointed to a nearly straight branch. "What about that one?"

"Too curvy." It was the fourth branch Nate had rejected.

Loretta put her hands on her hips. She smiled slightly. "What exactly do you expect to find in this forest?"

Nate pointed to a high branch that jutted out awkwardly. "There's my staff!" He looked around thoughtfully, "but how am I supposed to get it?"

"Watch this!" Loretta smiled and began playing a vibrant tune on her flute. Her music filled the air. Numerous small stones merged together to form the blade of an axe. She increased the intensity of her music. The blade floated up and struck the branch several times. The branch crashed down. Loretta slowed the tempo and the rhythm. When she finished her song, the gravel axe broke apart and the pebbles gently returned to the ground.

"That was brilliant," Nate marveled. He picked up the branch. "This is definitely the one," he exclaimed, breaking off the smaller limbs before standing as wizardly as possible. "How do I look?"

"Very noble." Loretta sounded like she was talking to a prince. "Now," her voice returned to normal, "we better get back to the clearing. Grandfather will be here soon."

"Thanks for your help today." Nate didn't want their time together to end. "I had a lot of fun."

"You're welcome, I had fun, too." Loretta rolled up the hem of her pants. "I'll race you back!" She bolted away.

Nate started after her. Jumping over a boulder, he easily passed her. "Looks like I'm going to . . ." He looked up and saw that he was about to collide with two entangled trees. He changed directions to avoid them. Loretta surpassed him.

"You can't catch me now!" Loretta taunted, dashing farther ahead of him.

"We'll see about that." Nate spied his chance. He ducked beneath a cluster of low-hanging boughs and felt as if he was coated with cobwebs from head to toe. *What did I run through?* Nate turned around. Merged with the shadow of the tree, a hunched ghostly figure stared at him with piercing red eyes.

"What are you?" Nate questioned, perplexed.

"I am a shadow warrior. Your life ended the moment you saw me," the figure declared in a low, eerie voice.

It unsheathed a glowing, green dagger, lunged forward, and drove the dagger deep into Nate's stomach.

The warrior withdrew the dagger. Nate screamed in agony and fell to the ground, paralyzed with intense pain.

Before the warrior could attack again, a delicate melody filled the air. Thousands of minuscule pink flecks of light surrounded the warrior, flashing brilliantly until the shadowy figure dissolved into nothingness.

"Nate!" Loretta screamed, rushing to his side.

With his head spinning, Nate glanced down. The area around his wound matched the hue of the bright-green dagger. The color was spreading. The pain was unbearable.

"Stay calm, Nate." Loretta held his head on her lap. She played three high-pitched notes on her flute. "Grandfather will be here soon."

Nate stared into Loretta's beautiful eyes and knew that somehow everything would be alright.

Chapter Twenty-Four

THE COUNCIL

A kettle hanging from the ceiling on delicate chains released a pungent, bright yellow steam. A silver counter the length of the wall was strewn with an array of canisters filled with powders, a mixture of bowls heaped with herbs, and an assortment of colorful needles varying in size.

Nate's torso was smeared with light-blue cream. He lay in the Halls' Medicinal Room listening to an elderly man with long grey hair and slanted eyes.

"You need plenty of rest," Dr. Jeely explained. "The cream stopped the poison from spreading but the shadow warrior's dagger is a cursed weapon. No amount of healing potion will work for that wound.

"Visitors will be allowed once you've been moved to the recovery ward. Now hold still." Dr. Jeely took three lengthy, thin needles off the table.

Gripping the side of the bed, Nate tensed.

"This won't hurt. It will just help you sleep." Dr. Jeely gently inserted the needles into the sole of his foot.

"You're right, that didn't hur . . ." Nate drifted off to sleep.

Dr. Jeely finished checking Nate's healing wound. "Your health has improved much faster than I expected, Nathanial." He looked at Nate through raised eyebrows. "I suspect that's a result of your friend's numerous visits."

"Oh, um, really?" Nate stammered. Bylo and Sadaki had visited occasionally, but Loretta had been there every day over the last few weeks.

"Yes, really." Dr Jeely smiled. "You are being released today. I'll leave while you change from your infirmary robe."

Nate rushed to his bag of personal belongings. He changed into his own clothes, slipping Blinkly's medallion over his head. He paced halfway across the room before there was a knock on the door.

"Come in," he invited anxiously. Loretta followed Dr. Jeely through the door. Nate felt like the room lit up.

"If your wound shows any abnormal coloring or increased sensitivity," Dr. Jeely instructed Nate, "come see me immediately."

"Yes, sir."

"If you're ready, Nate, Grandfather would like to see you."

"I'm ready!" Nate was tired of being confined in the recovery ward. They strolled down the hall. "Thanks for visiting me and making me study."

"I didn't let that shadow warrior get you. I couldn't let you die of boredom, either." She smiled. "Besides, I've enjoyed the company."

As they passed through a mirror, Nate slipped his hand into Loretta's. He was delighted when she squeezed it instead of pulling away. They walked in silence, hand in hand, until they reached Master Loperian's door.

"Will I see you at dinner?" Loretta met Nate's gaze.

"I'd like that." Nate squeezed her hand again.

Loretta pulled away slowly until only their fingertips touched.

When she stepped away, Nate let his hand fall to his side. He watched until she was out of sight before turning to knock on the door. The door did not open by itself. Master Loperian appeared next to Nate. Nate jumped.

261

"Sorry to startle you," Master Loperian greeted Nate. "I'm glad to see you're feeling better."

"Thanks, so am I."

"The Infinite Wizard is advancing south toward the Crimson City. The Council is in my office determining who can send aid."

"Are you sending me?"

"Only if he attacks Burrowville. King Siddon is not with the Infinite Wizard. It appears he has split his army but we cannot locate him. We believe you can help."

"Me? How?"

"Come with me and we'll explain." Master Loperian touched Nate's elbow. "Al—May—Bestafy."

Nate and Master Loperian appeared in the office. All the other mentors were seated around the seer stone. They nodded at Nate.

Within the stone, Nate was surprised to see faces floating in a blue mist, staring up at them. He recognized one of the faces and smiled.

"Welcome, Nathanial," the Red Wizard greeted warmly, his face growing three times larger than the others within the stone when he spoke. "I see you've recovered well."

"Yes," Nate replied, "thanks to Dr. Jeely."

"Has Master Loperian brought you up to date?" the Red Wizard asked.

"I've informed him about Versii and King Siddon," Master Loperian said, "but not about the quest we have for him."

"Nathanial, until we know the whereabouts of King Siddon," the Red Wizard explained, "our chances of winning this war are hindered. We believe the young elf who helped you at the Crossroads Inn was Princess Cenaya. If our assumptions are correct, she is in Wishington. Her mother wields the power of the Alamist which is our only hope in locating King Siddon."

"The Alamist?" Nate questioned.

"Yes," a face of an aged treeman responded. "It is the most powerful seer stone in the world."

The extremely wrinkled face of a woman dominated the mist when she spoke. "King Siddon has conquered the princess's land and we don't even know if the queen is still alive."

Master Loperian turned to Nate. "That is why we need Princess Cenaya. If you can convince her to join our efforts, she will be a mighty ally. Will you accept this task?"

All eyes were on Nate. "I'll do whatever I can to help."

"Your willingness is appreciated, Nathanial. You'll leave for Wishington with Sir Kilnipy in the morning," the Red Wizard explained.

Master Loperian turned to the Council. "Two of our mentors, Lady Kilnipy and Ei, will leave for Versii at once. Is everyone else clear on whom they are sending?"

"Yes," a chorus of affirmation came from the faces within the stone.

"Very well. We must remain united if we are to turn the tide of this war. Versii must not fall."

Nate was thrilled. He finally had a chance to prove himself.

Chapter Twenty-Five

HEAD IN THE CLOUDS

The next morning, Nate grabbed his knapsack and placed his wand in his boot. He started down the hallway. Rounding the corner, he bumped into Loretta. He beamed. "I was just on my way to see you."

Loretta grinned. "I thought you might need this." She handed him a smooth wooden staff.

"My staff? I thought the branch was lost."

"I know you did. I went back and found it so I could surprise you."

"Thanks!" Nate reached out and hugged her tightly.

Loretta looked up at him. "Do I get a kiss before you leave?"

Nate stepped back, momentarily speechless. Finally he uttered, "Of . . . c-c-course!"

Loretta closed her eyes, puckered her lips, and leaned toward him slightly.

Taking a deep breath, Nate stepped in closer, closed his eyes, and leaned in until his lips touched hers.

My first kiss! Nate opened his eyes and pulled back. He smiled broadly. Loretta giggled.

"What?" Nate felt his face flush.

"I'm sorry, it's just . . . well, you kissed me on the nose."

"Oh," Nate hung his head in embarrassment. "Sorry."

"That's okay." Loretta smiled tenderly and stepped forward. She cupped his face in her hands. "That just means we can try again."

She softly pressed her lips against his. Nate's heart leaped. They stepped back and grinned at each other.

Nate's smile faded. He didn't want to leave. "Sir Kilnipy is waiting for me. Will you walk with me?"

Slipping his free hand into hers, Nate and Loretta walked in silence until they reached the mirror.

"Please be careful," Loretta pled.

"I will." Nate embraced her one more time before he stepped through the mirror into the Griffin's Lair.

Atop the Halls of Magic, sunlight poured through open steel doors into the massive half-dome aviary. Two enormous griffins devoured fish while gremlins secured the last of their light armor, readying them for the trip to Wishington.

"Good, Nathanial, you're here," Sir Kilnipy greeted. "You'll be riding with Captain Galo." He pointed to one of the griffins. "Secure your items and climb aboard." He loaded his own supplies—which included a cauldron Nate felt certain he could sit inside comfortably—on the other griffin.

Nate had never flown before, but tried to appear confident. He placed his foot in the stirrup of a saddle large enough to hold two grown men. He slid his staff into a side scabbard, dragged himself up into the rear seat, and buckled his knapsack to the saddle just below his thigh.

"All ready?" Nate glanced nervously at Sir Kilnipy's griffin.

"Don't fret, Nathanial," Sir Kilnipy reassured. "Griffins can carry up to ten times their weight and fly extreme distances."

Captain Galo climbed into the front seat and grumbled, "You better strap yourself in good. I'm not coming back for you if you fall."

What little reassurance Nate had felt was dashed. He secured the seat strap around his waist as tight as he could, fastened the chest strap attached to the saddle's back support, and gripped the side handles.

With a loud whistle, Captain Galo pulled back on the reins. The griffin bounded out of the aviary and leaped into the air. They flew higher. With the wings' rhythmic beating in his ears and the wind in his face, Nate marveled at the expanding view. The snow-capped mountains behind them grew smaller. The dense forest below became a blur of green.

Before long, the excitement of the trip wore off. Nate's body began to ache and he shifted restlessly. When they finally spotted the sky castle in the distance, he was thrilled. High above the city, on a cloud illuminated by the blazing orange of the setting sun, the castle's diamond walls shimmered. Enchanted flames of different colors danced atop the palace's staggered turrets.

They prepared to descend. A rush of wind behind them was followed by an unexpected but familiar voice calling to Sir Kilnipy. Turning toward the voice, the griffins hovered in the air while a cumulus cloud plumped into the likeness of Master Loperian's head.

"Yes, Master Loperian?" Sir Kilnipy spoke to the cloud.

"The Infinite Wizard has diverted his course and is advancing on Burrowville at an unnatural pace," the cloudy Master Loperian spoke. "At this rate, the White Castle will be under siege by dawn. You'll have to find the princess another day. We need you in Versii at once."

"Yes, sir. We'll leave immediately."

"May you be blessed with safety and a swift victory." Another rush of wind returned the cloud to its original shape.

"Let's go." Captain Galo snapped his reins.

With great urgency, the griffins left the dazzling castle behind them and ventured across the Green Sea.

Flying through the night, Nate's mind raced. *Was his family safe? Could he help the Red Wizard? Would they save Versii?*

The sun peeked above the fluffy clouds below them. Captain Galo pulled Nate out of his thoughts. "The battle is right below us. Hold on tight."

The griffins descended rapidly. Nate braced himself, his heart pounded.

Chapter Twenty-Six

WAR

Emerging from the clouds, Sir Kilnipy, Captain Galo, and Nate were enveloped by a chilling, gloomy mist. Fighting a sense of uneasiness, Nate blinked several times while his eyes adjusted to the dimness. Captain Galo veered away from Sir Kilnipy with a sharp jerk, dodging a blast of flames.

Straining to see over his shoulder, Nate watched in horror. With rippling molten scales, a burgundy dragon whipped around, thrashing its spiked lava tail. A mighty swoosh of its smoldering, charcoal wings sent it bearing down on Nate and Captain Galo. The dragon's enormous eyes provided a window to its internal flames. Steam billowed from its nostrils. With another jolt, Captain Galo veered hard to the right, just missing the gnashing of the dragon's lethal teeth.

Captain Galo sent the griffin into a nose dive before sharply pulling up and to the left. They were unable to lose the dragon, but Nate lost everything in his stomach. Wiping his face, Nate looked up in time to realize Captain Galo was on a swift course to collide with a battle between several champions and harpies.

Nate searched for Ted among the champions. Captain Galo stormed through the harpies. Nate ducked to avoid a swipe from razor-sharp talons. Charging after them, the dragon bowled several harpies over in the air, sending them flying in all directions.

Captain Galo neared the outer wall of the White Castle. A spinner aimed directly at them launched hundreds of icy spikes into the air. Captain Galo swerved. The spikes embedded into the dragon. It let out a high-pitched bellow. Hurling to the ground, the dragon plowed into one of the countless squadrons of imps, carving a rut in its destructive path.

Captain Galo flew over the castle wall, circling until Nate pointed to where Sir Kilnipy had landed. "Over there."

Captain Galo touched down. Nate jumped off the griffin. He'd never been so happy to have his feet on the ground.

"Get your things so I can get back out there," Captain Galo demanded.

After grabbing his staff and pack, Nate helped Sir Kilnipy with the last of his supplies. The griffin riders rejoined the air battle.

Nate and Sir Kilnipy arranged a pile of wood into a pyramid and set the cauldron over the logs. Just then, the elementor, Ei, zoomed in as a massive fire blaze.

"Impeccable timing, Ei," Sir Kilnipy commended the blaze, handing Nate a long-handled wooden ladle. Ei torched the wood, transformed into a miniature cloud, and filled the cauldron with rain water. "Start stirring the brew, Nate." Sir Kilnipy emptied numerous pouches from his jerkin into the cauldron.

"If you don't need me anymore," Ei's face in the cloud spoke, "I'll rejoin the battle."

"We've got it from here," Sir Kilnipy acknowledged. Ei flew away. "Nate, you need to find the Red Wizard."

"Yes, sir." Nate passed the ladle to Sir Kilnipy and picked up his staff.

Suddenly, the outer gates crashed open. The cyclops brothers, Bilerd and Bowe, who had been valiantly attempting to secure the gates, were thrown backward into a battalion of soldiers. A Rider on a red-maned lion bounded past a massive battering ram. A horde of imps rushed into the courtyard.

Sir Kilnipy mixed the contents of the cauldron. He emptied one more pouch into the brew and stirred vigorously. Black smoke rose from the cauldron, morphing into two thick hands. Swelling as they billowed through the air, the hands pushed against the invaders, forced them back outside the castle walls, and reinforced the gates.

Nate raced through the courtyard in search of the Red Wizard.

"Nathanial!" Nate heard his name called over the crowd and recognized the voice.

"Father?" Nate spotted his father helping an injured soldier toward the inner gate. He bolted toward him, choking back tears. "You're all right! Where's everyone else?"

"Yer mother's in the keep and Denya's at the infirmary, both tendin' ta the wounded. Ted's out fightin'." He nodded to the sky.

"Have you seen the Red Wizard?"

"I haven't."

The wounded soldier spoke in a weak voice. "He received word the infirmary was about to fall so he went to their aid."

"Thanks," Nate said. "I'll be back soon, Father."

Nate rushed back to the cauldron. Sadaki and the old lady from the seer stone had joined Sir Kilnipy. Sir Kilnipy's continued stirring controlled the mighty hands.

"Glad you could make it," Sadaki greeted Nate, his voice confirming he was elated to be part of the war. Gesturing to the elderly woman by his side he added, "Nate, this is Baila."

"Thanks for coming," Nate said. Turning to Sir Kilnipy, he reported, "The Red Wizard is at the infirmary."

"The three of you must go there at once," Sir Kilnipy insisted.

Baila took charge. "We'll teleport together. Since we haven't been there, Nate, you'll have to concentrate on the infirmary. Sadaki, think of Nate while we chant the spell."

"Yes, ma'am," Nate and Sadaki agreed. They crossed their staffs in a triangle and touched each other's shoulders.

"Okay, Nate, focus." Baila nodded at Sadaki.

"Al—May—Bestafy!"

Nate and his companions appeared in a dim, smelly room. Nate and Sadaki steadied themselves.

Sadaki crinkled his nose in disgust. "Where'd you take us?"

"The undertaker's room." Nate grinned warily, covering his nose to defuse the smell. It definitely wasn't his favorite place but the room full of decorative coffins was the first one that came to mind.

"Where to now?" Baila asked, seemingly amused.

Nate pointed over his shoulder. "The front door is this . . ."

A blast shook the infirmary. The force of the explosion knocked all three of them off their feet. Nate slammed into a table. A ruby coffin fell to the floor, striking the edge of a nearby table. It caused a chain reaction. Dozens of coffins hit the stone floor and shattered. Shards and splinters flew. The blast caused a deafening noise to echo throughout the room. Nate shielded himself behind an overturned table.

The room became silent. Nate and Baila rose to their feet slowly. Nate surveyed the destruction in awe. Most of the coffins had been destroyed. Fragments of crystal, wood, and gems littered the floor. Several corpses were strewn about causing Nate to quiver. A gaping hole in the back wall of the infirmary smoldered. Smoke was filling the room.

"Is everyone alright?" Baila asked with deep concern in her voice.

"I'm fine." Nate coughed on some inhaled smoke.

"I'm fine, too. I think." Sadaki climbed out from behind a table and inspected himself.

Baila stepped forward. "Good. Get behind me. We've got company." The authority in her voice dispelled any hint of frailty.

A bulky imp with massive limbs climbed through the blasted hole. It glared at them and growled. Showing an abnormally wide mouth full of long sharp teeth, it swiped a long, barbed tail.

"Hysha—Untiria—Molderon—Erta!" Baila swirled her staff above her head. An enormous cyclone of water appeared in front of her.

Continually swirling her staff, Baila moved forward. The cyclone advanced, sucking the stout imp into its vortex.

The cyclone crashed through the gap in the wall, fully extinguishing the flames. "This way." Baila led them through the now larger opening.

Outside, the once-lush, beautiful grounds of the infirmary were withered, colorless, and overrun with nasty weeds. Nate almost didn't recognize it. Baila turned her cyclone on imps preparing to launch an explosive fireball from a sling. Sadaki rushed to the aid of a small band of infantry. Nate was rooted to the ground, staring at the magical battle raging in front of him.

Chapter Twenty-Seven

THE INFINITE WIZARD

With his tattered, grey robe billowing around him, the Infinite Wizard darted about wildly. Six black orbs spun around him haphazardly. The Red Wizard hovered in front of him, encircled by hundreds of miniature stars.

The Red Wizard thrust his staff forward. "Volus—Mayham—Abinigy—Rapum." A glass box encased the Infinite Wizard.

In the cramped space, the black orbs spun faster, becoming a blur of blackness. They expanded, shattering the box. Glass blasted the area, embedding into trees and striking nearby imps.

The Infinite Wizard sneered. "Ab—Balogy—Adoram—Senaral." An arsenal of axes, daggers, and spears hurled toward the Red Wizard. They struck the shield of stars, disintegrating upon impact.

Still hovering, the Red Wizard held his hand open in front of him. "Al—Meria—Balam—Falore." The stars in his shield combined into a petite ball matching the brilliance of the mid-day sun. The blazing sphere shot toward the Infinite Wizard only to be engulfed by the black orbs.

Just as the Infinite Wizard smirked, the diminutive sun exploded, rocking the infirmary grounds. The ensuing force knocked Nate to his knees. The Infinite Wizard shot out of sight. The

Red Wizard flew backward, hitting into the highest branches of a nearby tree.

"Rylam—Taham—Undra!" The Red Wizard yelled. His cape inflated, allowing him to float smoothly to the ground.

Suddenly, Nate saw movement in the trees. "Behind you!" he warned the Red Wizard.

The Wizard turned around a moment too late. A shadow warrior lunged from the shadows and drove his glowing, green dagger deep into the Wizard's chest. The Red Wizard fell to the ground.

The warrior angled for another attack.

Nate yelled, "Galo—Mafra—Octama!" With brilliance Nate had never seen before, an intense light flashed out of his staff. The shadow warrior dissipated. Hurrying to the Red Wizard's side, Nate could see the poison was already spreading.

"Hold on," Nate pled. "I'll get help."

"It's too late, Nathanial." The Red Wizard labored against the affects of the poison. "He's returning."

Following the Red Wizard's gaze behind him, Nate was horrified to see the deranged Infinite

Wizard in the distance, galloping through the air on a fiery horse.

"Sadaki!" Nate screamed. "I need you over here!"

Sadaki raced toward Nate. Baila froze her cyclone, suspending imps with their claws, tails, and other appendages protruding out of a newly formed giant ice sculpture.

She appeared next to Nate. "What is it, Nathanial?"

Sadaki rushed to his side.

Nate explained, "I've got to get help for the Red Wizard, but you have to protect him—from him." Nate pointed at the Infinite Wizard whose horse had landed and trotted toward them.

"We'll handle him." Baila glanced from the worsening Red Wizard to Nate. "You'd better hurry!"

Rushing back through the gaping hole in the undertaker's room, Nate dashed up the stairs. Following the moans of the wounded, he entered a room where numerous soldiers and townsfolk lay on tables, cots, and the floor. Scanning the faces of the few over-worked handmaidens, Nate searched for who he needed.

"Denya!" he called to his sister.

Denya placed an herb mixture over a soldier's gashed face, stopping the bleeding. "Nate? What are you doing here?" Her surprise was unmistakable. She rose and gave him a quick hug.

"I need your help. The Red Wizard's been stabbed by a shadow warrior and the poison is spreading. He needs the antidote."

"Follow me." Denya hurried across the hallway to the supply room. She flipped through a reference book. Grabbing a few jars off the shelves, she emptied the ingredients into a bowl. Stirring vigorously, she created a bright-pink mixture.

"That can't be right," Nate insisted. "It should be light-blue."

"I'm the handmaiden here," Denya defended. "How do you know?"

"From personal experience." Nate lifted his shirt slightly, revealing his healing wound. "Check the formula again. Hurry!"

"Fine!" Denya stole a concerned look at Nate's wound. He lowered his shirt. "Sorry, you're right; I should have grabbed the ahtoe dust instead." She grabbed a new bowl, remixed the ingredients, and produced a light-blue cream. "Where is he?"

"In the back, follow me."

Nate and Denya entered the hallway. The infirmary was rocked by another explosion. Nate fell to the ground. Denya braced herself against the wall, gripping the bowl. Pulling himself to his feet, Nate looked over his shoulder.

The infirmary's heavy, brass doors had been blown off their hinges. Several guards lay unmoving on the ground. A lanky elf Rider seated on the back of his red-maned black lion poised coolly in the doorway. Dressed in dark-mesh armor, the hood of the Rider's silver cape lay on his back, revealing a jet-black mohawk.

"G-g-go help the Red Wizard." Nate positioned himself between the Rider and Denya. "I'll take care of him."

"No way, Nate!" Denya cried.

"You have to." Nate locked eyes with the stone-faced Rider. The lion strutted casually over the fallen soldiers and moved toward them.

With his heart leaping in his chest, Nate pushed Denya away. "Get out of here! The Red Wizard needs you."

Denya bolted down the hall.

Nate pointed his staff at the Rider. "Galo—Mafra—Octama!"

The hallway filled with intense light, the Rider shielded his eyes with the crook of his arm. The lion roared and reared back. Sliding off the lion, the Rider landed awkwardly on his feet. The light faded.

"Stop him!" Soldiers scrambled from the adjoining hallway toward the Rider. The lion turned and pounced. With the soldiers struggling to defend themselves, the Rider took swift strides and swung his flail at Nate's head.

Jumping aside, Nate just missed being struck and slammed into the wall, dropping his staff out of reach. Falling to his knees, Nate pointed both hands at the Rider and yelled, "Ota—Esta—Nocafa!"

The minor gust of wind produced without the staff forced the Rider back only a couple of steps before fizzling out.

With a sinister leer, the Rider leaped forward, swinging mightily for Nate's head.

Nate dove to the side. The steel ball shattered the marble floor. Kicking the Rider's hands away from his flail, Nate pulled his wand from his boot and sat up. Picturing the night of the beast's attack, he concentrated and bellowed, "Snare—Eran!"

The dark-blue goo struck the Rider in the face. With a muffled scream, he fell backward, ripping at the substance that rapidly overpowered him. While the goo hardened, Nate turned his attention to the other hall and was relieved to see the soldiers had slain the lion. He raced downstairs.

Back outside, Nate found the Infinite Wizard gleefully hovering above the grounds. Near the gazebo, a thick chain binding Baila twirled her mercilessly in frenzied circles. Sadaki had been enveloped in the trunk of a tree that continued to grow around him. Only his face resembled his former self. A small band of soldiers formed a wall in front of Denya and the Red Wizard.

The Infinite Wizard yawned. He yelled, "Getta—Va—Ista—Maya!"

An unseen force slammed into the wall of soldiers, sending them flying over Denya's head. They crashed into the ground behind her. Holding his staff as a spear, the Infinite Wizard became rigid, shot down out of the sky, and landed in front of the barely conscious Red Wizard.

"Dontrud, ye fool. Ye had a chance to join us but ye have chosen death instead!" The Infinite Wizard pressed his staff against the Red Wizard's temple despite Denya's pleas for mercy.

Nate darted toward the Red Wizard.

The Infinite Wizard sneered. "Sima—Futa . . ."

"Snare—Eran!" Dark-blue goo struck the Infinite Wizard's staff, knocking it to the ground.

"Ye imbecile!" the Infinite Wizard shrieked, turning to Nate. "Ye must have a death wish too so we'll grant it to ye!"

Skidding to a stop, Nate shivered. He stared into the Infinite Wizard's multi-colored, speckled eyes and took aim.

"Snare—E . . ."

"Zamra." The Infinite Wizard snapped his fingers.

The wand exploded in Nate's hand. "Ow!" Nate screamed in pain.

"What a foolish master to send a boy to die!" the Infinite Wizard cackled.

Suddenly, dressed in full battle armor, Derik rushed through the hole in the infirmary wall. "Nate, catch!" He tossed Nate his staff.

The Infinite Wizard pointed his finger at Derik. "Ista—Ona—Fay!"

Derik screeched. Shrinking out of sight, he disappeared into his armor. Nate caught his staff in one hand and turned on the Infinite Wizard.

"Ota—Esta—Nocafa!" A strong wind gust slammed the Infinite Wizard into a tree.

"Is dat da best ye got boy?" The wizard staggered to his feet.

"Falma—Ottsa—Omstrafa!" A bolt of lightning blasted out of Nate's staff.

Shaking violently, the Infinite Wizard shrieked. Lightning coursed through his body. His hair stood on end.

Nate was hopeful the Infinite Wizard would collapse.

He stopped shaking and stood tall. "Better, but still not good enough." The Infinite Wizard sneered.

"Let's see what you think of this." Nate thrust his staff angrily toward the wizard. "Ala—Ontra—Hera—Jira!" Nothing happened.

"Tsk, tsk," the Infinite Wizard chided. "Forgetting yer spells already?"

Nate fought off panic.

The Infinite Wizard jeered. "Now it's my turn. Gana—Arna—Ola—Tisera!"

The Infinite Wizard trembled immensely and then transformed into a serpent with enormous bat-like wings. Three times longer than the wizard's body, the purple creature coiled up, ready to attack. Nate gawked.

"Let's see if we can bite his head off," the serpent hissed, springing forward.

Jumping aside, Nate dodged the attack. The serpent recoiled, preparing to strike again. Nate heard a loud crackling sound. The snake's head began to crystallize. To Nate's astonishment, the serpent shot up into the air, avoiding another ice blast and flew out of sight.

Nate glanced behind him.

Supported by Denya, the Red Wizard, with his bare upper body smeared in blue cream, stood with his staff pointed in the direction of where the Infinite Wizard had been.

Rushing to them, Nate helped Denya lower the Red Wizard to the ground.

With the Infinite Wizard gone, his black magic on the grounds had stopped. Baila pulled herself out from under a pile of chains. Sadaki begged someone to cut him free from the tree. Several soldiers hurried to his aid.

Nate suddenly realized changes around him. The sun shone brightly once again, the air had warmed, and the vegetation's natural colors had returned.

Nate approached his sister. "What happened to the imps?"

"They ran off just before you came out. That's why the soldiers were able to come and help me," Denya explained.

"What about the dead ones?"

"I don't know." Denya looked around.

"They melted," Baila explained. Nate hadn't seen her appear, but she'd clearly heard the conversation.

"Melted?"

"Yes, when the sun came out."

Nate glanced at the White Castle. "But the mist is still around the castle." *It doesn't make sense.* Nate replayed the battle at the infirmary in his mind. Suddenly it hit him. *Of course!* He knew how to save Versii.

Chapter Twenty-Eight

THE MISTRIDERS

Nate looked again at the mist surrounding the White Castle. His mind raced. "It's the Riders!" he yelled more to himself than to the others.

"Who?" Baila's confused look was unmistakable.

"The elves riding the lions," Nate explained. He looked from Baila to Sadaki, then to Denya. "They . . . they control the mist. Without the mist their army can't survive. We don't have to fight the army! We just need to stop the Riders."

"Are you absolutely certain about this?" Baila gripped Nate's shoulders.

"Yes." Nate knew he had their attention. "The mist disappeared after I killed the Rider here. In Blinkly's mural the imps didn't advance until the Riders did."

"Blinkly's mural? What are you talking about, Nate?" Denya eyed him with concern.

"No time to explain." Nate pointed at the White Castle. "We have to let the others know."

For a moment, Baila hesitated. "It's worth a try. I'll go to the castle, you three stay here. Sadaki, notify me at once if the Infinite Wizard returns."

"Yes, ma'am," Sadaki agreed.

"Al—May—Bestafy!"

After Baila teleported away, Nate and Sadaki gently moved the Red Wizard inside. Denya continued nursing the wounded in the triage area. Nate and Sadaki searched for others needing help. The trampled grounds were littered with debris. The surrounding wall had been reduced to rubble. The infirmary was riddled with breaches.

Nate passed the gazebo. "Help me!" He heard a faint croak.

"Help me!" the voice pled again.

Lifting a breastplate, Nate jumped back. Nestled within the armor, a hairy three-eyed frog stared up at him.

"It's about time," the creature snapped.

"Derik?" Nate lifted the critter in his hands. "I thought you'd vanished!"

"This is worse!" Derik insisted.

"Don't worry," Nate started toward the infirmary. "I'm pretty sure you can be fixed." He chuckled. "It just might take a little while."

"Denya," Nate called, entering the triage, "we need to help Derik."

"Of course." Denya turned from her patient. "Where is he?"

Nate lifted his hands toward her.

"Oh!" Denya studied Derik intently. "I can't help that!"

"What do you mean?" Derik squeaked.

"I mean," Denya apologized. "This is beyond my abilities, but I know someone who can. Follow me."

Leading them into another room, Denya approached a short man with white tufts of hair behind his ears. He squatted next to a miniature iron contraption encircled by glass and copper pipes. It sputtered and shook.

"Birchtran," Denya greeted him. "I've got another one for you."

"Denya, dear," Birchtran spoke. "I finally have some more ready." He finished filling a small bottle with pink potion and twisted a knob on the contraption before standing up. "It's the last one I can make here. Use it sparingly."

"I will, thank you." Denya took the potion. "This is my brother . . ."

"Of course, I know Nathanial!" Birchtran welcomed. "How can I be of assistance?"

"This is Derik." Nate nodded to the creature in his hands. "Can you help him?"

"Yeah, can you help me or not?" Derik demanded.

"My, my, my!" Birchtran clicked his tongue. "This will be a challenging patient." He grinned at Nate over his spectacles. "And not just because I have to heal him from the spell. Set him here." He motioned to a table covered with ingredients. "As soon as I find the purple moss, I'll get started."

Nate set Derik down. "You're in good hands, Derik. I'll check on you later."

Exiting the infirmary, Nate glanced toward the White Castle and sighed. He was sure he was right about the Riders, but the mist shrouding the castle was as thick as ever.

By late afternoon, he noticed a portion of the mist had started to vanish and he breathed his first sigh of relief. At sunset, he was encouraged. The mist around the castle looked splotchy.

Things were quiet at the infirmary, but Nate couldn't sleep. His thoughts jumped about all night. *What is happening at the White Castle? Was I right about the Riders? What if the Infinite Wizard comes back? Would Blinkly have figured this out sooner?*

The dawn broke. Nate looked at the White Castle and his heart leaped. The mist at the castle had vanished! *We did it Blinkly! I wouldn't have figured it out without your mural!*

A short while later, King Darwin arrived with his guards. Everyone was invited to join him in the triage room. Nate rushed inside, sitting on the floor near King Darwin.

"I'm grateful to see you regained control of the infirmary so quickly," King Darwin began. "At one point yesterday, I feared we would lose the White Castle. That changed when I was sought out by one of our allies named Baila. She shared a theory with me. If the elf Riders could be stopped, the mist would evaporate. The army would be forced to retreat.

"I was skeptical. When she assured me it had saved the infirmary, we spread word throughout the ranks to shift the main focus of the battle on destroying what we call the Mistriders. Their army seemed prepared for this very strategy. As soon as we changed our tactic, the entire imp army divided, surrounding each of the Mistriders. Gratefully, our soldiers were energized by the anticipation of saving the kingdom and fought with renewed zeal.

"True to Baila's theory, when a Mistrider was defeated, the mist dispersed and the army surrounding that Rider retreated. We had eliminated all but a few of the Mistriders when the purple moon entered the sky. Not knowing if the falling darkness would give the evil army the cover needed to renew their fight, we pulled everyone back to the inner courtyard.

"To our surprise, they never attacked. When daylight came, the sky was clear and the enemy was nowhere to be seen. A battalion of champions volunteered to confirm the enemy had left Versii. I have received word that they are fleeing to the Northern Fort."

I knew it! Nate wanted to leap for joy. He was right!

King Darwin looked at the crowd's awe-struck faces proudly. "All of you deserve my heartfelt gratitude. Your valiant efforts here at the infirmary led to the defeat of our enemy and this victory." The crowd cheered. "Please carry on your dedicated service. I must return to the castle to discuss our next plan of action."

Nate approached the king. "King Darwin? Sir."

"Yes, young man?"

"I'm Nathanial McGray. Where are Baila and the others from the Halls of Magic?"

"They are helping us repair the castle. The outer wall was nearly destroyed. Nathanial, you'll be happy to know that your family is safe and awaiting your return. We couldn't have won this battle without you and your friends." The king nodded and left to join his departing guards.

'Couldn't have won without you and your friends?' What does that mean? Does he know what I did?

Chapter Twenty-Nine

SACRIFICES HONORED

Nate pulled on his boots and looked around. His room at home was the same but life in Burrowville had changed.

His mother appeared at the door. "Are you ready to go, Nathanial?"

"I am." He stood and brushed off his clothes even though they were perfectly clean.

The McGray's made their way toward the castle. The damage to Burrowville was unbelievable. Homes along Center Street had been demolished. Crumbled bricks replaced shops along Main Street. The outer castle wall sagged, riddled with holes left from the barrage of destroyers.

In the chapel nearly filled with mourners, Nate took his seat next to his mother. Ted stood at attention with the other champions around Captain Goobler's casket. Nate couldn't remember ever seeing Ted look so serious. Each of Captain Goobler's three young children placed his sword, shield, and crossbow into his casket. They sobbed when the casket was closed.

Nate approached old Mrs. Goobler. He gently touched her shoulder. "I'm sorry for the loss of your son."

She turned to him. The sight of her tears made his heart ache. "Thank you, Nathanial." There was no grumpiness in her voice, only sorrow. "He appreciated your service to me."

Nate hadn't expected to hear that. At a loss for words, he gave her a light hug.

The funeral for Thorton Brades's oldest brother started shortly after. Thorton stared at the floor the entire time. Later that morning, there was a funeral for the elderly Mrs. Mungletuss. Her heart had failed while she made her way from their hotel to the castle with her husband.

After the funerals, Nate stopped in to see Lady Gordenall. No one was around and the house was empty. He rushed on to see the Red Wizard.

Sitting up in his infirmary bed, the Red Wizard explained Lady Gordenall's absence. "You'll see her again, Nathanial. She is safe, but in hiding. She left a parchment for you. I will get it to you when I am well enough."

Nate felt overwhelmed. Lady Gordenall was gone. Funerals were planned for every morning that week. Being surrounded by death made him miss Blinkly more than ever. To keep from getting depressed, he threw himself into the clean-up effort.

With the help of magic from Baila, the Kilnipy's, Ei, and Sadaki, repairs that would have taken several months were completed in just over a week. The reconstruction ended the same time as the funerals. On that day, two announcements came from the king. Versii had regained control of the Northern Fort and a grand memorial ceremony would be held in Burrowville the following week.

Nate handed Sadaki a folded parchment. "Please give this to Loretta." He longed to see her again. Sadaki and the other visitors from the Halls of Magic were leaving. Nate would return after the ceremony.

For the next week, countless Versiians poured into Burrowville. Nearly every available plot of land held at least one tent. There were three in the McGray's front yard.

The morning sun dawned the day of the memorial ceremony and Nate could feel the anticipation in the air. At the castle field, the platform for the ceremony jutted high above the mass of Versiians.

Ted scanned the field. A guard approached him. "Champion McGray?"

"Yes?" Ted turned in surprise.

"I've been instructed to escort you and your family to your seating area. Please follow me."

Exchanging looks of bewilderment, the McGray's followed the soldier to a roped-off sloped area near the platform.

"Wow, Ted!" Denya gushed when the soldier walked away. "What did you do to get us these seats?"

"Took down three dragons on my own." Ted acted as if he killed dragons every day before breakfast.

"Really?" Denya didn't mask the disbelief in her voice. She sat down next to Nate. Nate had heard the story many times over the last week, and he was equally skeptical.

"Well, maybe I had a little help," Ted admitted.

"A little!" A voice shrilled from behind Ted.

Nate recognized the competitor from the Shifty Desert.

"You wouldn't even be here if it weren't for me!" She stormed over to Ted.

"True. But that doesn't change the fact that *I* killed the dragons."

"You couldn't have killed them if you were dead!"

"Excuse me, Ted," their mother broke in. "Would you care to introduce us?"

"Of course," Ted replied sweetly. "Mother, Father, this is Eria. She's my defense support." He smirked playfully. "Eria, this is my family."

"Defense support?" Eria punched Ted hard in the arm. She took a deep breath. "It's a pleasure to meet each of you. I apologize for my outburst. Ted's ego is a bit too much for me. If you'll excuse me, I must return to my seat." Eria huffed off, retaking her seat with her back toward Ted.

"Good thing she likes me." Ted rubbed his arm and planted himself next to Nate.

"You're something else, Ted." Nate shook his head in disapproval. "That's no way to treat a lady. You should . . ."

A blast from a war horn drowned Nate out. It signaled the ceremony was about to begin. The crowd scrambled to find open spots to sit. King

Darwin stood regally atop the tall platform. The crowd fell silent.

Bracing himself on his elbows, Nate leaned back to stare up at the platform, listening intently.

"My fellow Versiians, thank you for joining me this day! We come together at a time of sorrow for the loss of our loved ones, a time of thanksgiving for our great victory, and, most importantly, a time of change! It's time to take this war to King Siddon!

"Over the next several months, we will work with our allies to gather supplies, build more war ships, and train all who are willing to fight with us. Our first objective is to reclaim the Kingdom of MaDrone!" King Darwin gestured to a band of centaurs and satyrs. "Our victory was aided by your valiant efforts.

"We also could not have won without our courageous and determined soldiers!" The crowd erupted in cheers. King Darwin waited for silence. "Today, we recognize a few of our soldiers who demonstrated utmost bravery. To present these honors, here are my captains."

In turn, the captains recognized outstanding soldiers under their command. When each soldier reached the platform, he or she received a golden medallion imprinted with the seal of Versii. Since all of the recognized soldiers had been seated in their area, Nate wasn't surprised when Lord Brade announced Ted's name.

Ted leaped to his feet and made his way up the platform stairs amid the cheering crowd. Ted had really killed *three* dragons. Eria Whiteheart was called next. Nate grinned. Lord Brade recognized Eria for keeping Ted alive while he killed the dragons.

King Darwin stood. "There are two final honors to bestow today. First, we recognize a young man whose heroism and ingenuity saved all of us from defeat. Nathanial McGray!"

In a daze, Nate glanced around at his astounded family. A sharp jab in his side pulled him from his trance.

"Don't keep the king waiting." Ted pushed Nate to his feet.

Nate moved as if in a dream. The king's voice seemed distant. "Nathanial McGray saved the Red

Wizard's life, heroically battled the Infinite Wizard, and discovered the secret surrounding the Mistriders."

On the platform, the captains and the Red Wizard, who'd regained most of his strength, each nodded to Nate respectfully. When he reached King Darwin, he gazed out over the gathered masses. Struck by nerves he had never before experienced, Nate could hardly breathe. His legs wobbled and he grabbed the wooden railing for support.

"Nathanial," the king declared, "you have proven yourself in battle and your worth to Versii. Do you swear to always fight valiantly, nobly, and loyally for Versii?"

"Of course!" Nate choked. *What's happening?*

"Kneel before me!"

Nate bowed down.

The king took a golden cloak from his squire. "Nathanial McGray," King Darwin draped the cloak around Nate's shoulders. "From this day forward you shall be known as the Golden Wizard of Versii!"

Nate gripped the railing and rose to his feet. His dream had come true. He was really a wizard!

Over the deafening cheers of the crowd, King Darwin instructed Nate to take his seat next to the Red Wizard.

Still in awe, Nate moved to a plush chair he hadn't noticed before and sank into the cushioned seat. He glanced from the grinning Red Wizard to the proud captains and then to King Darwin, who motioned for silence.

"I said there were two honors remaining today. Remove the veil!" In the center of the crowd, a white covering was pulled from a massive bronze sculpture.

"This monument," King Darwin continued as the audience stood for a better view, "reverently displays the faces of the Versiians and allies who have fallen in this atrocious war. It will stand in the castle yard, a constant reminder of their courage, and will give us the fortitude needed to continue fighting until we have defeated King Siddon once and for all!"

The crowd erupted with the most boisterous cheering yet. The war horn blared, declaring the end of the ceremony.

A pegasus landed on the platform. King Darwin waved to the crowd before mounting the noble steed and joining his escort of champions back to his castle.

"Congratulations, Nathanial," the Red Wizard praised Nate.

"Thank you." Nate felt like he had a permanent smile. "I didn't expect this today!"

"You've earned it. You were the key to our victory—and to my swift recovery I might add. You will still return to the Halls of Magic tomorrow. Even though you're now a wizard, your studies have not ended."

"Yes, sir!" Nate pictured Loretta.

The Red Wizard rose from his seat and took a letter from his robe. "Here is the letter Lady Gordenall asked me to give you. I'm sorry it took so long."

Nate stood and gratefully accepted the letter.

"See you in front of my tower at mid-day tomorrow." The Red Wizard chanted, "Al—May—Bestafy," and was gone.

Nate stared at the letter and sighed. *I wish Blinkly were here to see this.*

One of the king's advisors approached. He handed Nate a leather pouch. "Sir, here is your pay." He walked away.

Peering into the bag full of shiny gold bits, Nate was stunned. He was getting paid to learn magic! Fumbling slightly, he reclosed the pouch. Slipping the letter and pouch into his jerkin pocket, he slowly made his way to the bottom of the platform. His family was waiting.

His mother embraced him longer than usual.

Denya was next. Tears streamed down her face.

His father put his arm around Nate's shoulders. "I'm sorry, Nathanial. I should've been more supportive." He reached out and pulled Ted close with the other arm. "Ya've proved me wrong. I'm proud of both my sons."

"Thanks, father." Nate turned to him. "We couldn't have done it if you hadn't taught us to work hard."

Ted nodded his agreement. Nate thought he looked choked up.

"There's something I have to do," Nate said. "I'll meet you at home."

Making his way across the field, Nate humbly acknowledged numerous well-wishers. Someone stopped Nate with a slight bump on the shoulder.

Thorton toed the ground with his boot. "Congratulations, Nate."

"Thanks." Nate rocked on his heels. "I'm sorry about your brother."

"Me, too," Thorton choked. He turned away. Over his shoulder he added, "See you around," and disappeared into the crowd.

Arriving at the monument, Nate circled it reverently. There was Captain Goobler. General Triatun. Thorton's brother. His eyes fell on a familiar face in the back. Resting his hand on Blinkly's likeness, a lump rose in his throat. He pulled Lady Gordenall's letter from his jerkin.

Dear Nathanial,

I'm sorry I couldn't see you in person. Please don't lament my losses. War is a terrible yet sometimes necessary tragedy. If people like my husband and son weren't willing to sacrifice their lives, tyrants would rule our world.

King Siddon is moving forward mercilessly but he can be stopped. Although I haven't seen Danzandorian's medallion, I suspect it was given to him by his father. It may be important to the war effort. Until we meet again, please research it on your own in an attempt to determine its purpose.

I hope to see you at the Halls soon. Until that time, thank you for your friendship. Please remain safe and continue your wizardry studies.

Yours truly,

Lady Gordenall

Nate looked back at Blinkly's sculpted face. Flooded with emotions, Nate's tears flowed freely. He felt joy for their victories, sadness for the loss of lives, fear for the future war, but hope that King Siddon could be defeated.

Chapter Thirty

JUST THE BEGINNING

Nate was exhausted and slept soundly, waking later than usual the next morning. He enjoyed brunch with his family before they all boarded the wagon and set out to the Red Wizard's tower. Many of the visitors had left immediately following the ceremony. The town seemed deserted.

They approached a familiar street. An idea hit Nate. "Turn left, please."

"Why?" His father steered the horses around the corner.

"I need to see Mrs. Goobler." Nate pointed to her burrow.

Before his father came to a complete stop, Nate jumped off the wagon. "I won't be long." In his excitement, he banged on the front door harder than he'd meant to.

"Come in before you break the door down," a familiar, ornery old voice commanded. Inside the burrow, Nate found Mrs. Goobler in her rocking chair reading her books as usual.

"Sorry about that pounding," Nate apologized. He approached her. "How are you holding up?"

"As well as ever. I don't believe in letting discouragement get one down. But, what can I do for you?"

"Well, I remember seeing something like this in one of your books." Nate pulled Blinkly's medallion out from under his shirt. "I was hoping you could tell me what it is."

Mrs. Goobler slowly rose from her chair, reached out, and lifted the medallion. She examined it from every angle before releasing it with a gentle thud back onto Nate's chest. Walking more quickly to her bookcase, she scanned the book spines. "I believe I know exactly what it is." She pointed to the same book Nate had pulled down before. "Retrieve that for me."

Nate reached the hefty book and set it on the table. She flipped briskly through the pages. Nate watched anxiously. About halfway through the book, she stopped, leaving it open to the page Nate remembered.

"May I see the medallion more closely?" Mrs. Goobler asked.

Lifting it from around his neck, Nate handed it to her. She knelt down, raised it high in the air, and slammed the sparkling ruby against the stone floor.

Don't break Blinkly's medallion! Nate cringed.

"What you have," Mrs. Goobler declared, holding it high, "is a key." The ruby was now flush with the medallion's surface. The jagged edges of a golden blade protruded from the bottom.

"A key to what?" Nate asked, bewildered.

"To a treasure trove, of course," Mrs. Goobler explained. "Since the ancient times, dwarf clans built secret troves to protect their most valuable belongings. Medallions were forged to disguise the keys and entrusted to the head of the family. How did this medallion come into your care?"

"I was told to take it from a friend when he died." A tinge of sadness rang in Nate's voice. "Where would I find this treasure trove?"

"I'm afraid treasure troves are hidden by magic. They could appear as a tree or a rock, hidden in a lake, a desert, or a mountain. If you don't already know the location, they are nearly impossible to find."

"Oh," Nate muttered softly, staring at the key.

Mrs. Goobler struck the end of the blade on the stone floor, it retracted into the medallion, and the ruby once again jutted out.

"I wish I could've been of more assistance." Mrs. Goobler handed the medallion back to Nate.

"You were." Nate helped her to her feet. "At least now I know what the medallion is."

Nate returned to the wagon.

"Why so deep in thought?" his father asked.

"Oh," Nate's head snapped up, "just thinking about something Mrs. Goobler said. She really is a remarkable lady."

At the base of the tower, Nate gathered his belongings and bid farewell to his family.

The Red Wizard was waiting. "Ready?"

Nate nodded.

He took Nate's elbow. "Al—May—Bestafy!" They appeared in the Wizard's quarters. "The past few weeks have been a remarkable journey for you." The Red Wizard motioned for Nate to sit in the plush, crimson chair. "Your journey isn't over just yet. Before you return to the Halls of Magic, you must go to Wishington. You will meet Sir Kilnipy at the city entrance tomorrow afternoon."

"But how . . ."

"First, you need another one of these." The Red Wizard handed Nate a healing potion. "As you well know, this potion doesn't heal everything, but it's good to have in emergencies. I want you to study this." He pulled *Dontrud's Collection* from the bookshelf. "This book contains all of my favorite spells. Most of them will be too advanced for you at this point, but you'll be able to master them in time."

"Thank you, sir." Nate placed the book and potion in his pack.

"As you know, Wishington is too far for me to teleport you, but you need to get there quickly. I've decided to send you there with a friend." The Red Wizard whistled softly and a three-headed creature squeezed through the bedroom door.

"Demon!" Nate ran to the animal, rubbing each of its heads as they licked him.

"Demon will follow your directions exactly as long as you have the Idiom Talisman." The Red Wizard motioned to the ring on Nate's finger. It was the ring Marian had given him when he arrived at the Halls of Magic. "You don't have to worry about getting lost, Demon knows Zndaria better than most." The Red Wizard paused meaningfully before continuing, "Now that you are the Golden Wizard of Versii, you will be expected to do great things. Study extra hard so you are prepared when we summon you."

"I promise." Nate stood tall.

"It is time for you to go. Travel safely and don't forget who you represent."

Rubbing Demon behind the ears, Nate climbed on, secured his staff to his pack, and held Demon's mane tightly. The Red Wizard opened the window shutters.

"Take us to Wishington," Nate commanded.

Trotting over to the window, Demon leaped out, freefalling before opening his massive wings. The breeze pushed Demon upward. With a few powerful beats of his wings, Demon took Nate high into the mid-day sky.

Eyeing the miniature images of Burrowville below, a broad smile crept across Nate's face. "I did it!" he yelled triumphantly, "I really became a wizard!"

Nate soared into the horizon, excited for his new adventure—an adventure that was just beginning.

♦ The Golden Wizard ♦

Nate's adventure continues in

Scroll 2
The Alamist Queen

For more information and release date
visit us at:

www.zndaria.com

♦ The Golden Wizard ♦

About the Authors

Jerry D. and Stephanie R. Jaeger have been married for 17 years and are the proud parents of four wonderful children. Throughout their lives, they have proven that with hard work and persistence, any dream is possible.

Jerry struggled with stuttering and was bullied in school. His mother told him he could accomplish anything. He earned his black belt in Kempo Karate when he was 18 years old. He graduated with a history degree from Brigham Young University and a law degree from the University of Wyoming. Fulfilling one of his biggest dreams, he served as a special agent for the FBI. Jerry currently works as a prosecutor for Washington County, Utah, has completed two marathons, and is training for the Ironman 70.3.

Stephanie's parents taught her the value of hard work and encouraged her to pursue her education. Taking this advice to heart, she earned her undergraduate accounting degree from the University of Wyoming and master's degree from Southern Utah University while raising her family. Successfully balancing family and work, she ran her own accounting practice for several years. One of Stephanie's proudest achievements is recently finishing a marathon with Jerry.

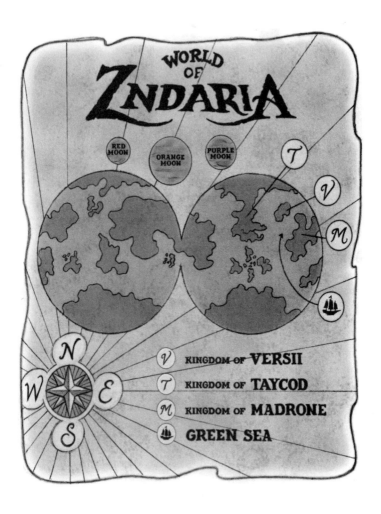